JEDI QUEST

THE TRAIL OF THE JEDI

JEDI QUEST

CHOSEN BY FATE.
DESTINED FOR CONFLICT.

#1 THE WAY OF THE APPRENTICE

#2 THE TRAIL OF THE JEDI

SPECIAL HARDCOVER EDITION: PATH TO TRUTH

JEDI QUEST

BY JUDE WATSON

THE TRAIL OF THE JEDI

LUCAS BOOKS

SCHOLASTIC INC.

New York   Toronto   London   Auckland   Sydney

Mexico City   New Delhi   Hong Kong   Buenos Aires

www.starwars.com
www.starwarskids.com
www.scholastic.com

No part of this work may be reproduced, stored in a retrieval system, or transmitted in any form
or by any means, electronic, mechanical, photocopying, recording, or otherwise, without written
permission of the publisher. For information regarding permission, write to Scholastic Inc.,
Attention: Permissions Department, 557 Broadway, New York, NY 10012.

ISBN 0-439-33918-9

12 11 10 9 8 7 6 5 4   2 3 4 5 6 7/0

Printed in the U.S.A.
First Scholastic printing, May 2002

JEDI QUEST

THE TRAIL OF THE JEDI

From deep space, the planet Ragoon-6 lay concealed by a blue mist shimmering in the midst of a cluster of stars. As the transport descended, the mist broke into sparkling particles that swirled around the viewscreen. Then the ship broke through into a planetary atmosphere so clear it seemed as transparent as water. Glinting below was a planet as green as a flashing jewel.

Anakin Skywalker's breath caught as he leaned forward. He had never seen such a beautiful approach to a planet.

Obi-Wan Kenobi put a hand on Anakin's shoulder as he, too, leaned forward. "I had forgotten how beautiful it is."

Anakin glanced at his Master. Despite his beard, his face suddenly looked young, even younger than when Anakin had met him five years before, when Anakin was nine years old. Obi-Wan had been a Padawan then, just like Anakin was now. No doubt Obi-Wan was remembering his other trips to the planet, the ones he had taken with his own Master, Qui-Gon Jinn.

Wren Honoran, their Jedi pilot, nodded. "I always forget until the next time I see it. It takes your breath away every time."

"It's amazing that it hasn't been colonized," Anakin said.

"It was given in trust to the Senate by its own government," Obi-Wan explained. "Only small tribes of natives still inhabit it. A Senate committee handles requests to visit. Only the Jedi and small groups of beings can visit at any one time. Access is strictly controlled. That way Ragoon-6 will remain unspoiled, as the government wanted. There are no air lanes, no factories, no cities."

"The Ragoons never allowed colonizers to settle," Wren said. "Their own population sickened and dwindled until finally there was only a handful left. They could no longer keep out all those who wanted to come. They knew they would have to give up what they loved most in order to save it."

"But if they'd just allowed colonizers to come, they could have kept their planet," Anakin pointed out.

"Yes, but they chose not to. The beauties of their

world were too important to them," Obi-Wan explained. "To keep the planet unspoiled was their first goal."

"They sound selfish to me," Anakin said. "They wanted to keep their planet beautiful for themselves and a few others."

"Or perhaps they were wise," Obi-Wan said. "It is not for us to say."

Anakin turned his gaze back to the planet's surface and sighed under his breath. One of the hardest things he found about becoming a Jedi was suspending judgment. To Anakin, things were good or bad, smart or stupid. Obi-Wan had this maddening way of not taking a stance on things.

"If I had a planet that was truly my homeworld, I wouldn't give it away. I'd want to be able to come back whenever I wanted," Anakin said. He had spent his early years on Tatooine, but he had been a slave. He did not feel as though the planet was his home, even though his mother still lived there.

"The Temple is your home," Obi-Wan said gently.

Anakin nodded, but he knew that in his heart he did not feel that way. He loved the Temple and was always glad to return to it. He loved its order and its grace. He loved the beauty within it, the Room of the Thousand Fountains and the deep green lake. But it did not feel like home.

Unlike the other Jedi students, Anakin had once had a home. Unlike them, he remembered his mother. He remembered running home through the heat and bursting through the door to be met with cool and shade and open arms. He remembered his warm cheek against her cool one. . . .

No, his home had not been a planet. It had been smaller, and humbler, and much more precious.

Life in that home had not been easy. There had been times of food shortages, times when they had shivered at night for want of fuel.

The Temple was never short of food or fuel. The temperature was maintained at the optimum degree for the various beings who lived within. It was warmer and safer than the slave quarters on Tatooine.

But it still didn't feel like home. *Home will always be where Mom is. No matter how old I get. No matter how long it's been since I've seen her.*

"There are the Rost Mountains," Wren said. "We'll land and I'll say good-bye there." He grinned over his shoulder at Anakin. "And then you'll try to catch me."

Wren was an older Jedi with a graying beard who had chosen to teach at the Temple rather than continue to go on missions. Anakin had studied the politics of governments with Wren, and he knew the Jedi Master had a wide-ranging grasp of political philosophies in the galaxy. As part of his Jedi service, Wren also volunteered to take part in training missions for Jedi teams.

Anakin and Obi-Wan would try to track Wren through the wilderness. The exercise was designed to strengthen the bond of trust between Master and Padawan. On Ragoon-6, they would have only each other to depend on as they tracked Wren through the rugged terrain.

Anakin's eyes danced as he bowed respectfully to Wren. "It will be my honor and pleasure to find you in a single day, Wren."

"Ah, in only one day, you say. You are almost as cocky as your Master used to be," Wren said. "I think my clues just got harder. I enjoy teaching lessons to overconfident Padawans."

Anakin hid his grin. In his classes, Wren had been respected, but he'd also been teased behind his back by the Jedi students for taking himself a little too seriously. Anakin would love to find him before a single day had passed. That would deflate his superior manner a bit!

Still, Anakin couldn't help wondering why Obi-Wan had decided to take him on this training exercise. He already trusted his Master with his life. They had been on difficult missions together. He had known him since he was a boy. Every mission brought them closer. Why did they have to take a detour for what seemed to be an elaborate game?

They skimmed over a meadow lush with wildflowers and tall green grass. Above the grassy field, snow-capped mountains hugged the tiny meadow. The sky was deep blue streaked with violet. Anakin could almost smell the fresh scent of the flowers. He had never seen such a lush world with so many vivid colors.

Wren landed the craft expertly in a sheltered spot tucked into the rocky side of the mountain. He accessed the landing ramp and turned to them. "Remember, you must leave your comlinks aboard ship. No homing devices or droids can be used. You must rely on each other and the Force."

Anakin and Obi-Wan nodded. They both knew these things, but it was part of the ritual that Wren repeat them. They placed their comlinks in Wren's hand, and he stowed them in the secure storage bin.

"If you can't find me, we will meet back here in ten days." Pausing only to sling a survival kit over his shoulder, Wren nodded a good-bye. "May the Force be with you." His gray eyes twinkled. "You'll need it."

Wren ran lightly down the ramp. He swung himself up on a flat rock, then jumped to another. Within moments, he had disappeared.

"Wren is certainly looking forward to puzzling us," Obi-Wan observed.

"He really should get out more," Anakin said.

Obi-Wan turned to Anakin. "Do you think Wren is taking this too seriously?"

"No," Anakin said hesitantly. "But I don't understand why a Jedi Knight would want to spend his time this way when he could be on missions."

"Wren has been on hundreds of missions," Obi-Wan said with a frown. "He has served for most of his life. Now he wishes to give back his knowledge to the Padawans. It is a noble gesture."

Noble, but boring, Anakin thought.

He thought it better not to share the thought with his Master. "How long do we give him?" he asked instead.

"Just a few hours," Obi-Wan answered. "Time enough for us to explore the surroundings a bit and have a meal, you'll be glad to hear. We'll be on rations and protein cubes once we leave, but we can raid the ship's galley now." Obi-Wan gave Anakin a piercing look. "This is designed to teach us, Anakin. But it is also supposed to be fun."

"Of course, Master." Anakin didn't want Obi-Wan to think he wasn't looking forward to the exercise. He knew Obi-Wan had been here twice with Qui-Gon and treasured the memories. Anakin wanted to have that same experience with his Master.

Obi-Wan heated up a meal for them, which they ate sitting in the meadow surrounded by flowers. The morning sun was a brilliant yellow, casting its warmth on Anakin's skin. He ate quickly, anxious to start the day.

"Qui-Gon and I tracked a Jedi named Winso Bykart," Obi-Wan said, pushing aside his plate and leaning back on his elbows. "It was our second trip to Ragoon-6. On the first trip, we had to cut the exercise short. I didn't know why at the time, but Qui-Gon had received a disturbing vision about Tahl."

"I have heard about her," Anakin said. "She was supposed to be brilliant."

"She was. Brilliant and funny and kind. She was unique." Obi-Wan looked out over the meadow. "She was a great friend of Qui-Gon's. I don't know if he ever truly accepted her death."

"But a Jedi must accept death," Anakin said. "It is part of life."

"Yes," Obi-Wan said quietly, his gaze still far away. "That was the difficulty for Qui-Gon."

What do you mean? Anakin wanted to ask. But something stopped him. Sometimes, when Obi-Wan spoke of his Master, he became distant. Anakin could tell by the expression on his face. He did not want to intrude by asking prying questions.

Silence fell between them. Anakin was used to that. Usually their silences felt comfortable. This one was not. Anakin watched Obi-Wan's face. He saw the quiet yearning there. Obi-Wan was missing Qui-Gon. And for the first time, it bothered Anakin.

He wasn't feeling jealous of Qui-Gon, Anakin told himself. It wasn't that. He had loved Qui-Gon, too. Something else was bothering him about his Master's preoccupation.

Maybe it was because he was still envious of their relationship. Obi-Wan had taken Anakin on as his Padawan with reluctance. Anakin had always sensed that. Qui-Gon had believed in him, and Qui-Gon's belief had influenced Obi-Wan. How could Obi-Wan ignore his beloved Master's dying wish?

Anakin had thought himself lucky at the time. To arrive at the Temple already chosen by a Jedi Knight! It was unheard of.

Now that he was fourteen, he had seen his fellow Jedi students wait and hope to be chosen by a Jedi Knight. He had talked to his new friend, Tru Veld, about it. Tru had told him about how his Master, Ry-Gaul, had studied him. Tru had felt Ry-Gaul's eyes on him during lightsaber matches, during classes, even walking around the Temple. They had shared many conversations together. When Ry-Gaul had officially chosen Tru at last, he had felt honored.

Anakin too had always felt honored to be Obi-Wan's Padawan.

But why? Anakin suddenly wondered. *Obi-Wan did not choose me.*

Today, for the first time, Anakin saw the difference.

Then a new thought pierced his heart. Had Obi-Wan brought him here as a desperate act, to develop a closeness he did not feel?

CHAPTER TWO

Obi-Wan didn't dwell on the past. It was not the Jedi way. But his Master was still part of his life, more a constant companion than a memory.

On Ragoon-6 it was hard not to drift back to the past. On his first visit here, Qui-Gon had received a vision that Tahl was in danger. He had not told Obi-Wan. They had left abruptly and had ended up going after Tahl against the wishes of the Council. In that dangerous mission, Qui-Gon's vision had come true. Tahl had died. But not before Oui-Gon had risked everything, including his way on the Jedi path, to declare his love for her.

These were all things Obi-Wan had not known at the time. Some of them Qui-Gon had told him later. Others Obi-Wan had realized himself. Qui-Gon had never spoken of his love for Tahl. It was a place within him too deep for Obi-Wan to go. He was not invited there.

Now he had a Padawan, and he understood Qui-Gon's sense of privacy. There were things it had been better for him not to know.

But how do you know what to share with your Padawan, and what to keep to yourself?

There were times when Qui-Gon's silence had annoyed or hurt him. Yet in the end, it had not mattered. Nothing had mattered except the bond between them.

He wanted to have this bond with Anakin. He knew it would develop over time. Why was he in such a hurry to make it happen? Something was driving him on, but he did not know what it was. It was as though Anakin would slip out of his grasp if he did not secure him. He had to do all the right things, the way Qui-Gon had done.

Obi-Wan thought back to his second visit to Ragoon-6. It had been close to the time he and Qui-Gon left for Naboo on what would become their last mission together. But on Ragoon-6 that ending was far away. They had enjoyed the tracking exercise, the time together, the break from their missions.

For even then, they had known that the galaxy was changing. Missions were more numerous. Trouble spots erupted constantly. The Senate called for their help more often. It had been difficult to find the time for the training exercise, but Qui-Gon had insisted on it. He had promised Obi-Wan that they would return to Ragoon-6. When Obi-Wan had pointed out that they had plenty of time, a fleeting look of deep sadness had crossed Qui-Gon's face.

"It seems there is always time when you are young," he'd said. "But you cannot hold a moment, Padawan. It runs out like water in your fist. You must seize it when you can, even as it falls away."

Obi-Wan could have kicked himself. He thought at the time that he had reminded Qui-Gon of Tahl. He had, he supposed, but now he also knew that Qui-Gon was thinking of how fast time could pass, and how crowded a life could become.

Remembering this had spurred Obi-Wan on to slot the time for this visit with Anakin. It hadn't been easy. The Jedi Council needed Master–Padawan teams. Yet Yoda and the Council were always careful to grant a request for this training mission. They had seen how many times it had strengthened the ties between a Master and an apprentice.

Would it strengthen theirs? Obi-Wan hoped so. He knew Anakin wasn't looking forward to the exercise as he was. Anakin wanted to be doing serious things. He was anxious to prove himself on missions, anxious to see the galaxy. This time together would be a pause before a future Anakin was eager to meet. Obi-Wan hoped that the exercise would not be too tame for someone as gifted as Anakin.

That was why he had asked Wren to participate. Anakin might smile at how seriously Wren took his role, but he would soon appreciate how challenging Wren's cleverness could be.

Obi-Wan stood. "Come, Padawan. It is time to go."

They took off in the direction Wren had gone. At first, the tracking was easy. Wren had not bothered to hide the clues that a Jedi would catch — a disturbance of leaves on the forest floor, the slight indentation of a heel. After two hours, they were momentarily stumped when they could not locate his direction, until Anakin plucked a silver-gray hair from a leaf, and pointed.

"This way," he said, self-satisfied.

Behind Anakin, Obi-Wan shook his head. Sometimes he felt that there was so little he needed to teach his Padawan. Even to Obi-Wan, who knew him so well, Anakin's command of the Force could be astonishing.

Wren had better come up with his most clever tricks, or Anakin would follow through on his promise and find him by nightfall.

*   *   *

By midday, Anakin and Obi-Wan had to admit they were lost. Wren's clues had grown increasingly difficult, and Anakin's cocky confidence had hardened into dogged resolution.

Frustrated, Anakin suddenly stopped. With one smooth motion, he swiped a rock and tossed it into the woods. It hit a tree with a satisfying thud.

"Feel better?" Obi-Wan asked.

"No."

"I didn't think so. Frustration is part of this exercise, young Padawan."

"I know, I know," Anakin muttered. "Breathe in my impatience. Then let it go."

"Correct," Obi-Wan said serenely. He waited a moment. "Well?"

"Well, what?"

"I didn't see you breathe." Obi-Wan knew he was straining the patience of his Padawan. Yet these small tests were good lessons.

Obediently, Anakin shut his eyes. He took a breath and released it. He opened one eye. "Can I stop now?"

"I suppose." Obi-Wan grinned. "If Wren could see you now, he'd be very happy."

A gleam of humor lit Anakin's eyes. "The day isn't over yet."

"Come on, let's backtrack," Obi-Wan suggested, heading back down the trail. "We must have taken a wrong turn."

Dappled sunlight streamed through the thick leaves overhead. They moved from pools of light into shadows and back again. The sun warmed their skin, then the shadows cooled it. The air smelled fresh and softly scented. It was a good day to be lost.

Anakin suddenly crouched down and examined the trail. "He stopped here." He pointed to the dirt on the trail.

Obi-Wan bent down. "Yes, I think so."

"Definitely." Anakin's voice rose in excitement. "And then he passed over the grass here. This way."

He led the way off the trail into the forest. Obi-Wan noted the clues and followed. After a morning of looking for tiny changes in the ground and leaves overhead, Wren had left a substantial clue to his progress. It must be part of his strategy to mix up his hard clues with some easier ones.

Anakin led the way through the dense forest. It was easier to track Wren now. The ground was soft and the leaves underfoot were still wet. Obi-Wan allowed Anakin to take the lead, enjoying the fragrant walk through the trees.

Anakin stopped and turned. "There's a clearing

ahead," he said in a hushed tone. "And some caves. Do you think we've caught up with him already? Those marks still look fresh."

"I doubt it," Obi-Wan said. "But proceed carefully. We have to get close in order to end the exercise."

"A lightsaber's length away," Anakin said. "But I think our only chance is to surprise him."

"Anakin —"

Obi-Wan's call was swallowed in the shadows. Anakin ran silently ahead, then dashed out into the clearing.

Obi-Wan followed, wishing he could teach his Padawan to curb his impatience.

He wished this even more when he realized where Wren had led them. They had stumbled on a malia den.

He remembered the malia from his first trip to Ragoon-6. They were fast, agile, deadly creatures, fierce predators with triple rows of teeth.

Anakin stood frozen in the middle of the clearing. He had seen the malia spread out on the rocks. At first their blue-gray fur had melted into the shadows.

At least they hunt at night.

He had fought them with Qui-Gon. He remembered the gleam of fluorescent green eyes, the cunning of the creatures as they circled. He did not want to meet up with them again.

"What are they?" Anakin whispered.

"Just . . . back . . . up. . . ." Obi-Wan murmured.

But even as they took two steps backward, Obi-Wan saw one creature stir. A long, tapered snout lifted. Two fierce eyes opened. A low rumble deep in the malia's throat told Obi-Wan that they were in trouble.

CHAPTER THREE

The malia sprang at the same time as Obi-Wan. The creature was just a blue streak in the air. Obi-Wan slashed at it and it fell with a wounded howl.

The rest of the pack rose. Obi-Wan counted swiftly. Sixteen. But there could be more in the caves. They were lean, rangy creatures. One malia stepped forward and lifted its snout. Its eyes flashed as it bared its triple row of yellow teeth.

"Attractive creatures," Anakin said, his lightsaber at the ready.

"Back up slowly. Perhaps they won't attack. But if they do, don't underestimate them," Obi-Wan said rapidly as he backed up a step. "I fought them with Qui-Gon. They have very quick reflexes. They will come at us from the trees. They will try to separate and surround us."

Anakin took a cautious step back. "How did you defeat them?"

"We didn't," Obi-Wan said. "A native tribe helped us."

"You needed *help*?" A flicker of nerves crossed Anakin's face.

"Yes, Anakin. Even Jedi need help occasionally. So just keeping backing up . . . very . . . very . . . slowly. Oh, and another thing. Don't look them in the eye."

"Oops," Anakin said.

The snarling pack surged forward. Obi-Wan saw a streak of blue as two malia separated from the others and headed for the trees. Another dodged to come at Anakin from his left.

"Anakin —"

"I see it —" Anakin almost stumbled, surprised by the burst of speed the malia took on as it pounced. He barely got his lightsaber lifted in time to slash at the creature's neck.

Obi-Wan made sure his Padawan had succeeded even as he tracked another malia that was circling toward him from the left. At the same time, he kept his gaze roaming in the trees, where two malia were jumping from branch to branch. "Whatever you do, don't let any get behind us," he said as he leaped toward the malia, brandishing his lightsaber. The malia retreated, snarling, its eyes a flash in the shadows.

Anakin whirled to fend off two malia that were attempting to get behind him. At the same time, another malia dropped from the tree.

Obi-Wan leaped toward him to help his Padawan. Back-to-back, the two of them fought the snarling pack.

The air seemed to be full of flying fur and pointed yellow teeth. The malia attacked in a fury. Obi-Wan and Anakin had to use their feet to kick, as well as their lightsabers. Anakin was not yet able to easily use the Force to move living objects, but Obi-Wan was able to send several malia flying with his outstretched left hand.

They continued to back away into the forest. Now they could use the trees as barriers. Anakin fought furiously. The rhythm of the battle took over his actions. His lightsaber was a red blur in the shadows, and his body became a weapon as well. He leaped, kicked, and whirled. He sent a malia flying with a well-timed chop of his hand to the animal's windpipe. A strangled snarl ended in a yelp as the malia flew backward and hit a tree.

There were now eight malia left, half the original pack. Two were limping from the battle. The others circled, snarling. They still bared their teeth and howled at the Jedi, but Obi-Wan could see that their attack had become less focused. They had not expected such resistance.

Next to him, Anakin was breathing hard. His lightsaber was held firmly in his hand. Not even the slightest tremble betrayed how hard he had been working.

"Let's keep backing up," Obi-Wan murmured. "Slowly. Do not look at them directly."

Anakin gritted his teeth. "Believe me, Master. I won't make that mistake again."

The malia continued to follow them, but kept a few meters away as the Jedi retreated. Obi-Wan did not blame the malia for the attack. The Jedi had stumbled on their territory. He did not want to wipe out the entire pack.

The Jedi speeded up their pace a bit. The malia did not follow. They huddled together and roared their anger as Obi-Wan and Anakin retreated. The shadows gradually swallowed them up, and soon all the Jedi heard were their angry snarls.

Anakin shivered as he deactivated his lightsaber. "The sound alone is enough to scare you," he said. "Do you think they'll follow us?"

"I doubt it. Despite their cunning, they are simple creatures," Obi-Wan said. "They were defending their home. We were lucky that it was daylight. They weren't in hunting mode."

"You mean they would have fought harder?" Anakin asked incredulously.

"And longer." Obi-Wan tucked his lightsaber back in his belt. "They would not have given up."

"And here I thought this was such a peaceful planet," Anakin remarked. "Why would Wren lead us into a malia den? That seems extreme, even for Wren."

"He wouldn't," Obi-Wan said. "We must have mis-read the clue. Let's return to the place on the trail where we saw it."

They quickly moved through the trees, retracing their steps. They bent over the clue once again.

"It was my fault," Anakin said. "I saw the grass flat-tened at the edge of the trail, and I assumed it was Wren." He carefully searched the surrounding ground as Obi-Wan continued to study the disturbance in the dirt.

Anakin was right — it was an impression of a heel. Wren had put too much weight on his foot, enough to leave a mark. It indicated that he had stopped here for a moment. It was an easy clue for the Jedi to follow. Wren had not bothered to try to conceal it or make it harder to read.

It wasn't like him. Then again, maybe it was. Wren enjoyed being inconsistent.

"Master — this way," Anakin called. "This time, I'm sure."

Obi-Wan crossed to the opposite side of the trail.

Here, the level ground dropped sharply to a steep rocky hillside.

"Look, here. And here." Anakin left the trail and leaped down the slope from rock to rock. "He went this way."

Obi-Wan followed. It was important to let Anakin lead. That was part of the point of the exercise.

Anakin made his way down the steep slope, his footing sure and swift. They reached the bottom of the slope and immediately plunged into a forest so thick that the overhanging branches shut out all light. They paused for a short moment so that their eyes could adjust. The trees were tall, with long, flat leaves and vast trunks with thick, peeling bark. Anakin began to study the ground again.

Obi-Wan searched without moving, his gaze traveling over the dirt, rocks, and surrounding trees.

Frustrated by his inability to find a clue, Anakin straightened and began to study the trees around them. He hurried forward to a tall trunk and leaned in to examine it.

"He rested here. He touched the trunk with his finger."

Obi-Wan saw the slight flaking of the bark near Anakin's pointing finger. "How do you know? All the trees here have peeling bark."

"There is sap running alongside. Here's a finger-print. Smudged. But it's there."

"Yes. So he went — which way?" Obi-Wan enjoyed the keen look in Anakin's eyes.

With the trunk of the tree to guide him, Anakin eagerly searched the ground again. "This way!" he called triumphantly. "We'll catch him yet!"

Smiling, Obi-Wan followed Anakin through the forest. This was what he'd hoped for. Anakin had forgotten his impatience with the exercise and what he'd thought was his secret feeling that it was a waste of time. He was now filled with the excitement of the chase.

They moved through a thick curtain of needles and bark. They could no longer see the mountain looming over them. It was as though they were tucked away in a fragrant green cave.

Then the trees stopped abruptly and they came upon a sheer rock wall. The wall curved around them and rose on three sides. There was no way to go except back the way they'd come.

"It's a dead end," Anakin said, disappointed. "But I was so sure Wren came this way!"

"Hold on," Obi-Wan said. "Look around you. You might be missing something. Remember your Temple exercise to explore the present moment? Close your eyes."

Anakin closed his eyes. Obi-Wan waited until he was sure his Padawan had focused. "What did you see?"

"Bark and leaves under my feet. Sheer wall ten meters ahead with insufficient handholds for climbing. Small plant growing in one crevice thirty meters up. Snow dusting at top of cliff. Bird circling twenty degrees to my right. At the base of the rock wall, what appears to be a small opening — a den of a small animal, or —" Anakin's eyes popped open. "A cave."

Obi-Wan smiled. He had seen the entrance to the cave minutes before. "Let's see what it is."

Anakin and Obi-Wan examined the small opening. "It's not as small as it looks," Obi-Wan said. "It could be the nest or den of an animal."

"It looks like it opens up," Anakin said, peering inside. "Let me go in."

Obi-Wan hesitated. He would rather be first. But part of this exercise was also for the Master. He had to learn to let go, to allow his Padawan to test his skills. He knew Anakin was well trained and could handle what lay beyond.

"All right, Padawan."

Without a glow rod, Anakin would have to feel his way. He eased inside the hole carefully, one hand on his lightsaber hilt.

Obi-Wan heard Anakin's voice echo hollowly. "It's a cavern! It's beautiful!"

Obi-Wan squeezed inside the hole. It was a bit more difficult for him to make it. He wondered how the tall, stocky Wren had managed.

He was able to straighten after crawling just a few meters. Anakin stood ahead of him, scanning the cavern.

It truly was beautiful. The walls shimmered with phosphorescence, lighting the space. The cliff face outside had been gray, but this stone was pink with veins of bright gold and silver. Cone-shaped deposits of the stone hung from the ceiling and rose from the floor.

The smooth floor sloped steeply downward. Anakin hurried ahead, running his hand along the wall. "He'll never expect us to find him in here."

Obi-Wan took a deep breath, testing the air. It smelled fresh. There was most likely another opening in the direction they were headed. Wren had probably left the cavern by now.

The air smelled damp as well. That was normal in a cavern. Pools of water sat in the depressions of the stone floor. Some of them quite deep . . .

"Anakin!" Obi-Wan snapped his Padawan's name. His voice echoed, but Anakin had run ahead, around a corner, and hadn't heard. Obi-Wan picked up his pace.

He rounded the corner. Anakin had paused before another opening to the cavern. This one was larger and began above Obi-Wan's shoulders. Through it they could see only a patch of blue-and-violet sky. Against the shimmering pink and gold of the walls it was a breathtaking sight.

"Anakin, we should get out of here," Obi-Wan called as he quickly made his way toward his Padawan. "I think this cavern may flood periodically."

Anakin nodded and waited for his Master to catch up. Just then Obi-Wan heard a noise. A slight *whoosh* sound. He moved faster. Anakin turned back to the opening.

"It's so beautiful," he said in a hushed tone.

The *whoosh* grew louder. Now it was a roar.

"Hang on!" Obi-Wan shouted as a wall of water suddenly blocked out the sky and headed straight toward them.

CHAPTER FOUR

Anakin desperately clung to a ledge as the water rushed into the cavern. The force of it battered him against the cavern wall. Another wave entered, and the water went over his head. The shock of its coldness almost made him lose his grip.

He fumbled for his breather with one hand while he hung on with the other. He began to feel light-headed as he struggled to attach his breather with one hand. Spots swam before his eyes.

He managed to insert his breather and inhaled deeply. He felt strength flow back into his muscles. Still, his body was being pummeled by the furiously rushing water and battered against the cones and the wall of the cave. He had to get out or he would drown.

He glanced back. He could barely see his Master, who

was clinging to a rock hanging from the ceiling. As Anakin watched, Obi-Wan transferred his grip to the next cone. Fighting the rushing water, he pulled himself forward.

Anakin grabbed the ledge a short distance away. He pulled himself forward, too, every muscle straining with his effort. He reached for the next handhold. Then the next. He fought for every centimeter.

At last he felt the smooth curve of the cavern entrance. He paused there, holding on against the violent water, waiting for his Master. After a few moments, Obi-Wan pulled himself up next to Anakin. He pointed up. They would have to let go now and try to get to the surface. Anakin nodded.

Anakin rolled his body into a ball and rested his feet against the cavern wall. He closed his eyes, gathering his strength and the Force. When he felt the Force enter him, he pushed himself off the cavern wall.

The power of the water almost battered him back against the wall and swept him inside the cavern, but Anakin fought it with all his strength, swimming up, trusting that air and sunlight were above.

After a few meters, the pull of the water lessened. He was able to make headway against it. He saw a lightening above. Sunlight. He swam toward it eagerly. The dappled patterns seemed to beckon him.

He burst above the surface of the water. Ahead he

saw a booming waterfall, spilling down from a cliff above. That was the source of the powerful current both above and below the surface. Anakin waited until his Master broke the surface and then struck out toward the bank.

He pulled himself up onto dry land. He ripped the breather from his mouth and gasped for breath. Water streamed off his clothes and the ends of his hair as he bent over, gathering his strength. Beside him, Obi-Wan was doing the same.

"The malia den, and now this," Anakin said when he could speak. He shook his head, sending water droplets flying. "Did I misinterpret the clues, Master? They seemed so clear."

"No, I think we went the right way off the trail," Obi-Wan said. "But we shouldn't have gone through the cavern. Jedi clues are designed to be difficult, not life-threatening."

Anakin flushed. It was his fault. In his impatience to impress his Master, he had rushed into the malia den and into the cavern.

But Obi-Wan wouldn't say anything. That was the trouble. It was worse for Anakin to have to wonder what his Master was thinking.

Obi-Wan scanned the surrounding area. "No doubt Wren used a cable launcher to vault the cliff face."

"But I didn't see any marks above," Anakin said. "Wouldn't the launcher have scarred the rock face?"

"Let's return and examine the cliff again," Obi-Wan decided.

"I'd rather not take another dip," Anakin said with a shiver.

"We can climb the hill here," Obi-Wan said, scanning the steep incline that rose from the bank. "That will bring us on top of the cliff overlooking the cavern."

They climbed up the steep incline, occasionally using their cable launchers. The sunlight dried their clothes and hair and warmed them as they climbed high above the water. At last they reached the top of the cliff.

Anakin stood at the top. From here he had a commanding view of the waterfall below and, in the distance, the valley. Still more mountains rose behind him.

He turned and found the overlook to the forest's edge below. It didn't take him long to find where Wren had been.

"Look, Master. He was here," he said, pointing to a place where the grass was flattened. "He could have been watching from above while we stood there."

"Possibly," Obi-Wan said. "There was no way for him to know that the cavern would flood, I suppose."

"At least we know for sure that we have him," Anakin said. His Master still looked uncertain. "Don't we?"

"Let's follow the trail," Obi-Wan said.

Anakin moved to track Wren's progress over the top of the cliff. A trail led into the mountains, and he began to trudge up it.

He could sense that his Master was uneasy. Something was bothering him. But Obi-Wan did not confide.

He never does, Anakin thought. *How can we get closer if he keeps all his thoughts to himself?*

He had to speak or he would burst. Anakin stopped and turned around. "You never tell me what you're thinking," he said.

Obi-Wan stopped. "You should be careful when you use words like 'never' and 'always,' Padawan," he said. "Things are rarely so absolute. You should be more precise. Clarity of mind is important for a Jedi."

Another lesson. Must there be so many? "Yes, Master." Anakin turned and continued up the mountain. He had only gone a few meters when he realized that Obi-Wan had never addressed what he'd said.

That's because he knows it's true. He had perfect communication with Qui-Gon, and he knows he can never achieve that with me.

He had been right all along. This exercise was a waste of time.

The trail rose higher, and the temperature began to drop. The sun still warmed them, so they did not need their thermal capes. But above, Anakin could see the snowy peaks, and he knew if they kept climbing at this rate, they would encounter snow by dusk.

Anakin felt shivers on the back of his neck. But it wasn't the temperature. Something was wrong. He tested the feeling. The Force was like a net, closing around him. The trees seemed to hang over the trail, menacing them. The sky seemed lower.

We're being watched.

And whoever it was, it wasn't another Jedi.

Anakin glanced at Obi-Wan. He did not move his head, only his eyes, so that if someone were watching they would not see even a wordless communication. Obi-Wan's gaze told him everything he needed to know. He, too, felt the presence of someone.

Obi-Wan stopped, and Anakin did the same. "We should split up," he said in a tone loud enough to carry, but not too loud to be obvious. "We're getting nowhere. I'll head back, and you continue ahead."

"Yes, Master." Anakin knew that Obi-Wan would double back in order to trap whoever was following them.

Obi-Wan moved back down the trail, and Anakin continued on. He did not feel fear or alarm. He felt ready for whatever would come.

He reached out to the Force beyond the trail, beyond

his immediate surroundings. He took in the planet in a way he was learning to do.

There was darkness here, but the feeling was confused. He could not pinpoint why or how the Force was affected. *That was the trouble*, Anakin thought ruefully. He could access the Force easily. Interpreting it was another matter. At such times he fully realized why he was still a Padawan, and not a Jedi.

He was on a switchback trail now that hugged the mountain as it rose. As Anakin turned a corner, the trail behind him would disappear. The rocks rose steeply on his left and a sheer drop was on his right. If he met whoever was following him, the battle would be tricky. And how would Obi-Wan manage to set up an ambush on this kind of terrain?

Anakin was busy thinking these thoughts when he turned the next corner and saw the flash of a weapon. It was held by a young woman in a gray cloak that blended with the rocks.

"Don't come any farther," she said in a clear voice. "I promise you, I know how to use this. And it is aimed straight at your heart."

CHAPTER FIVE

Anakin waited. The Force was around him, rising up from the ground beneath his feet and the forest below. It was not strong in the girl. Anakin guessed she was close to his age. She was afraid, he suddenly knew. He felt her fear ripple out and touch him, as clearly as if she had put out a hand.

And he felt something else — his Master was near. Obi-Wan was above him. He needed to keep the girl's attention on him.

"Why do you want to shoot me?" he asked in a reasonable tone.

"Do not try to trick me," she said. "I know you've been following me. I know you killed my friends and my teacher." Now her voice wobbled slightly. "I won't let you kill me, too."

Anakin saw a blur above. It was his Master, leaping down from the sheer cliff above.

Obi-Wan dropped behind the girl and disarmed her in a move so fast she did not have time to turn or even take a breath.

Obi-Wan tossed the weapon to Anakin.

"You know how to use a *hydrospanner*?" Anakin asked in disbelief.

"I didn't have a real weapon," she said in a small voice.

"Were you threatening to kill me, or fix my speeder?" Anakin asked. He couldn't believe he had been fooled by a hydrospanner. What kind of Jedi was he?

In answer, the girl suddenly whirled and tried to throw herself down the sheer drop. Obi-Wan had antici-pated the move and simply reached out with one hand and stopped her.

"That's not a solution," he said. "We're not going to hurt you. Maybe we can even help you."

Anakin took a few steps closer. "What happened? What do you mean, somebody killed your friends?"

The girl pulled her cloak around her. Her hood fell back, and waves of long blond hair spilled down her back.

"My name is Floria," she said. "I'm from the planet Aaeton, only half-day's journey from here. Young people from my planet often go on survival camping trips on

37

Ragoon-6 when we reach fourteen years of age. We have a special allowance from the Senate because we gave the elders of Ragoon refuge when they handed the planet over to the Senate. My group arrived yesterday. I was separated from them. We were on a hike and I got lost." Floria's eyes suddenly filled with tears. "When I returned . . . I . . . the ship . . ."

"Go on," Obi-Wan prompted.

She swallowed. "Was completely burned," she said in a whisper. "I knew we were supposed to meet back there for the evening meal. I am afraid my friends and my teacher were in it. Someone blew it up."

"You're sure they were inside?"

She twisted her hands together. "How can I be sure of anything? Everything was smoke and ash and fire. Maybe they escaped. Maybe they are lost. I've been searching ever since. But lately I am positive that some-one has been following me. They were keeping just out of sight."

"More than one being?" Obi-Wan asked.

"I — I'm not sure," Floria stammered. "I don't know what's wrong. I just know that something is. And I'm all alone!"

So I was right about the darkness in the Force, Anakin thought. *Something is wrong on this planet.*

"Dry your tears," Anakin said gently. "You're not alone. We will help you."

"Who are you?" she asked. "And why would you help me?"

"Because we can," Obi-Wan said. "Now, the first thing to do is examine your ship."

The ship was just as Floria had described it — a charred hulk.

"Stay here with her," Obi-Wan told Anakin. He disappeared inside the remains of the ship.

He emerged a few minutes later, his face streaked with ash. "There are no remains of beings aboard," he said.

Floria closed her eyes in relief for a moment. "Thank you for looking."

"This is a small cruiser," Anakin said, looking at the ship. "It's for travel within a planetary atmosphere. How did you get here from Aaeton?"

"We have a space cruiser in orbit," Floria explained. "We're supposed to rendezvous with them in three hours. But I have no way to contact them to tell them we won't be there." She brightened. "Can you take me? I can tell them what happened, and they'll send a rescue party down."

"Of course," Obi-Wan said. "We'll have to hike to our cruiser, but it's not far."

"Thank you," Floria said. "I feel certain now that my friends are alive. But they could be in danger. We must find them."

Obi-Wan drew Anakin aside. "Something dark is present on this planet. Can you feel it?"

Anakin nodded. "Yes, Master. But it is unclear."

"There seems to be different energies operating," Obi-Wan said. "It is unclear to me, too. We must be on our guard." He frowned. "I have been thinking about Wren."

"What about him?" Anakin asked.

"The clues we have been following . . . something is wrong. They are too easy, and they lead us to danger. Maybe Wren isn't the one leaving them." Obi-Wan gazed up at the mountain. "Something might have happened to him."

CHAPTER SIX

You never tell me what you're thinking.

Why hadn't he answered his Padawan? Instead, he had corrected him. Obi-Wan's mind churned, and his heart felt heavy. He did not know why he had deflected Anakin's feelings, but he knew he had been deeply unfair to his Padawan.

Anakin could speak so easily of his feelings. He often spoke without thinking, often spilled out exactly what was in his heart. It was behavior that was not like a Jedi.

And I correct him. Is that right?

Obi-Wan knew why Anakin was this way. It was because of Shmi. Anakin's mother had given him a great gift. She had given him an open heart. His feelings were deep and spontaneous. That was a good thing. But they sometimes led him to act too fast, to make quick judgments.

He is the opposite of me, Obi-Wan thought. *It has always been difficult for me to speak what is in my heart.*

Anakin had been wrong to say he never told him anything. Obi-Wan only held back what he thought Anakin did not need to know, just as Qui-Gon had done with him. Obi-Wan had begun to suspect that Wren's clues were not right, but he felt it was better for Anakin to discover this on his own. He could see that Anakin's eagerness to find Wren was clouding his judgment. Perhaps Anakin was being less careful because he was not on a mission, but an exercise.

These were things it was not proper for a Master to share with his Padawan. Yet Anakin wanted Obi-Wan to share everything.

Sighing, Obi-Wan led the way back to their ship. He would have to think of a way to bring up what had happened. He knew he had hurt Anakin's feelings.

Obi-Wan knew the terrain by now and led them down the mountain and across rocky hills and meadows so they would not have to double back, which would have cost them time. Within two hours, they were hiking across the meadow toward the cliff face where Wren had docked the ship.

"Don't worry," Anakin said reassuringly to Floria. "We have a comm unit aboard ship, so — Master! Look at that. It's beautiful . . ." Anakin frowned, sensing something was wrong.

Obi-Wan saw the fine blue mist heading for them. "Anakin, move!"

Anakin's reflexes were perfect. Without thinking, he leaped to one side as Obi-Wan vaulted toward Floria. He grabbed her and jumped, accessing the Force.

The spray hit the ground where Anakin and Floria had been standing.

"Stokhli spray stick," Obi-Wan said. "Keep moving."

"A what?" Floria asked.

Another burst of spray headed their way. Obi-Wan jumped again, still holding Floria against his side, as he tried to pinpoint the location of their attacker.

"It's a weapon," Anakin explained as they ran toward cover. "It sends a spraynet mist with a stun current. You don't want it to hit you."

"I guess not," Floria muttered as Obi-Wan gained the shelter of some boulders and pushed her behind them.

"We have to circle around and stop whoever is doing this," Obi-Wan said to Anakin. "Stay here, Floria."

She gazed at him with wide, frightened eyes. "Don't worry. Just come back again."

"If you head for those trees, I'll circle around the boulders and see if I can surprise the attacker," Obi-Wan told Anakin. "Remember, the Stokhli stick has a range of two hundred meters."

"Makes it hard to get close enough with a lightsaber," Anakin said.

"Exactly," Obi-Wan murmured. "Just leave that to me. Keep the attacker busy. And don't take chances!"

"Yes, Master."

Anakin ran out from the shelter of the boulders. Obi-Wan waited for a moment until he saw the spray of the Stokhli stick spew into the air. Anakin Force-jumped, and Obi-Wan could see that the spray would miss him by centimeters.

His Padawan's reflexes and timing were extraordinary. Anakin had timed his move so that the spray would miss him, but by so small a margin that the attacker would be diverted and want to attack again. His concentration would stay on Anakin.

Obi-Wan bent over so he could keep the shelter of the boulders as far as possible. He ran around them, then timed his move to the second attack on Anakin. He dashed across the open meadow toward the screen of trees.

He made the trees without an attack. Now the rest would be tricky. Anakin would keep himself just out of range of the Stokhli — he hoped — but Obi-Wan's objective was to get close enough to disarm the attacker. That meant he would have to be squarely in the stick's range.

Obi-Wan took off through the trees, heading toward where he had last pinpointed the attacker. No doubt the attacker would keep moving, especially when he or she realized that Obi-Wan was gone. He would count on Anakin's skill to prevent the attacker from moving too far or too fast.

Soon Obi-Wan stopped. He concentrated, accessing the Force to become one with the environment around him. The sounds of the forest dropped away. He did not hear the rustle of leaves in the wind, the occasional scurry of a small animal, the rub of a branch against another. He only heard the slight *ssiiing* sound of the spray stick.

Thirty degrees to his right. Obi-Wan moved carefully now, moving behind tree trunk to tree trunk. He barely touched the ground as he moved, making no sound.

Sssing! Another attack from the Stokhli stick. Coming from a few meters to the right of where he'd pinpointed the attacker.

Now Obi-Wan moved quickly, running over the soft ground, his boots silent, his breathing so controlled he made no sound.

He saw the attacker ahead. It was a male Tursha. Obi-Wan saw the distinctive headtails and the eleven-fingered hands lightly holding the Stokhli stick. The Tursha was just behind the tree line.

Obi-Wan drew his lightsaber and jumped. The Tursha turned, his Stokhli stick spewing mist. Instead of leaping to the side, Obi-Wan jumped high. He anticipated that the Tursha would move the stick in a sweeping motion to cover as much air as possible, and he did. Obi-Wan sailed over the mist, his lightsaber high.

The Tursha had fast reflexes. He moved back, putting himself in the open, past the tree line. Obi-Wan saw Anakin leap toward him.

Obi-Wan came down. He kept his lightsaber away from the Tursha. He did not want to kill or injure him. He wanted answers.

Anakin's lightsaber was drawn as well. The Tursha moved a fraction, enough so that the spray from the stick would put Anakin securely in range. Obi-Wan moved fast. He leaped again, this time adding momentum in midair in a Jedi method that never failed to surprise opponents. He kicked out with one foot at the handle of the stick. He gave his blow topspin, and the stick flew out of the surprised Tursha's hand and then twisted in midair. Though Obi-Wan didn't plan it this way, the spray hit the Tursha full in the face.

He fell to his knees. He gazed out in shock at Anakin and the meadow beyond.

"They . . . were . . . mine," he managed to gasp out, before the spray paralyzed him completely. He slumped against a tree trunk, his face frozen in a surprised expression.

CHAPTER SEVEN

"Who is he?" Floria asked in a hushed voice. She tiptoed closer, keeping behind Anakin.

Obi-Wan bent over the inert form. He examined the Tursha's utility belt and searched the hidden pockets in his cloak.

"I'd guess he's a bounty hunter," he said to Anakin. "He has a variety of weapons and what looks to be some false ID docs." He took a restraining device from the bounty hunter's belt and secured him to the tree.

"You'll recover from the stun in about five hours," he told the Tursha, who could do nothing but stare straight ahead. "But I guess you know that. We'll return for you."

"Can't you ask him what happened to my friends?" Floria asked.

"He can't speak. Not yet. If he did attack your

friends, we'll escort him to your home planet for trial," Obi-Wan said.

Suddenly, tears spilled down Floria's cheeks. "He killed them," she said. "I know it. Did you hear what he said? 'They were mine.' He did it."

"You don't know that," Anakin told her soothingly. "He could have meant any number of things. We don't know anything about him. You can't jump to conclusions that way. You can't imagine the worst."

Anakin patted Floria's shoulder as she used the hem of her cloak to dry her tears. Despite his reassuring words, he was worried. He had felt the growing darkness on the planet. Floria could be right. Her friends could have been attacked.

Obi-Wan stared out at the meadow, thinking. He did not acknowledge Floria's tears, or try to soothe her in any way. Anakin couldn't believe it. How could Obi-Wan be so cold?

Obi-Wan signaled to Anakin and drew him aside. "What is a bounty hunter doing on an unpopulated planet?" he asked. "Why would he attack us? Is he here for another purpose? Why would he attack a group of young students on a camping trip? It doesn't make sense."

"But they've disappeared," Anakin said. "Something happened."

Obi-Wan eyed the Tursha. "I wish I could ask him some questions. I'd like to know if he's operating alone."

"We're running out of time," Anakin said. "Floria's group is supposed to rendezvous with the space cruiser in less than an hour."

"You are too focused on Floria's problem," Obi-Wan rebuked him. "There is a larger issue here, and possibly more important things at stake. What is happening on this planet? We won't find out if we leave."

"We have to leave," Anakin said. "We promised Floria."

"We promised to help her," Obi-Wan said. "I'm not sure what that will entail. Not yet. Have you given no thought to your fellow Jedi? What if something happened to Wren?"

"We don't know that," Anakin argued. "And we do know that something happened to Floria's friends. So I say we go with what we know. Aren't I supposed to tune into my feelings?"

An odd look passed over his Master's face. "Your feelings are important, Padawan," he said kindly. "And they are important to me. But you are being swayed by emotion. That is different from following your feelings. You should know the difference by now. Gather the Force around you. See what it tells you."

Annoyed at Obi-Wan's rebuke, Anakin turned away.

He gazed at the trees, letting the tones of green invade him, letting the noise of the rustling leaves calm him. He gathered in the Force.

Once again, he felt the darkness rise. Once again, it seemed to be coming from several sources. Yet there was one powerful darkness here as well.

Surprised, he turned to Obi-Wan. "It is confusing. There seem to be several sources of darkness, and at the same time, only one."

Obi-Wan nodded. "That is what I sense, too."

"But I don't get any feeling about Wren. Perhaps he is in danger," Anakin said reluctantly. He didn't want Obi-Wan to be right.

"Let's go to the ship," Obi-Wan suggested. "We'll try to raise Wren on his comlink. Then we will make the decision about Floria." He put his hand on Anakin's shoulder. "Together."

Anakin nodded. He realized that Obi-Wan had just given him a kind of apology. It was just like Obi-Wan to veil it in lessons.

They returned to the girl, who had slumped on the ground a good distance away from the bounty hunter.

"Come on," Anakin said. "We're heading for the ship."

"Good." She rose with a shiver. "I can't wait to get off this planet."

"One moment. We can't leave the Tursha like this,"

Obi-Wan said. "When dusk comes, the malia will be roaming." He withdrew a flexible tarp from his survival pack. He unfurled it and created a free-form tent around the seated bounty hunter. The color of the tarp took on the color of its surroundings, camouflaging the Tursha. "This should protect you somewhat," Obi-Wan told him. "We will return for you before the paralyzer wears off."

They left the trees and struck out across the meadow. Anakin hoped they would be able to raise Wren on the comlink. He was anxious to bring Floria to safety. Suddenly their training exercise had turned into a mission. He didn't mind the shift. He would rather face danger and save lives than track an elder Jedi up a mountain any day.

They were relieved to see that the ship was just as they'd left it. They hurried toward it.

Suddenly, the ground in front of them exploded, sending a shower of dirt and rocks into the air. Another explosion came to the right of them.

They were being fired on — from all directions at once. The blaster bolts pinged and whistled, sending up showers of dirt around them.

Anakin and Obi-Wan both activated their lightsabers in one fluid motion.

"Get Floria to the ship!" Obi-Wan yelled, deflecting fire.

Anakin tucked Floria against his side, away from the worst of the fire. He ran quickly, deflecting fire as he moved.

Obi-Wan stayed in front of him, taking the brunt of the fire and clearing a path to the ship. Anakin activated the landing ramp and quickly ran up with Floria. After a moment, Obi-Wan followed.

Anakin slid into the pilot's seat. "We don't have time to contact Wren. We'd better get out of here."

"Yes, hurry!" Floria's face was white with fear. "What if they come after this ship, too?"

Obi-Wan peered outside at the blaster fire that was still erupting. Bolts peppered the ship. Smoke filled the air outside.

Anakin reached for the engine controls.

"Wait." Obi-Wan's voice was a command.

"Wait?" Floria's voice rose. "For what? To get killed?"

"I feel a surge in the Force," Obi-Wan said.

"You feel a what in the what?" Floria's head whipped from Obi-Wan to Anakin.

An explosion outside the ship almost threw Obi-Wan to the floor. Floria screamed and gripped her chair. "Please, let's take off!"

Obi-Wan gripped the console, concentrating, as though there were no blasters, no explosions outside. And now Anakin could feel it, too. The dark side surged.

He had been too intent on leaving, on Floria's panic, on the blaster fire. This was something he had to learn. His connection to the Force was strong, but sometimes it got crowded out by more immediate things. Obi-Wan was able to hold everything in his mind at once.

Obi-Wan dropped to his knees. Floria looked down at him as though he were crazy.

"Is he afraid?" she whispered to Anakin. "I don't blame him! Let's take off!"

"Wait." Anakin watched Obi-Wan. He knew now that the darkness was in the ship, not outside it.

"I found it." Obi-Wan's voice was muffled, and Anakin had to strain to hear over the sound of the blaster fire.

Obi-Wan raised his head, then stood. He held a black box in his hand. "A sleeper bomb. If we had taken off, we would have been blown out of the sky."

CHAPTER EIGHT

Floria looked as though she might faint. "A bomb? Can you d-defuse it?"

"I'm afraid not," Obi-Wan said. "It could go off at any time. So let's go."

"The comlinks —" Anakin said.

"No time. Go!" Obi-Wan ordered, leaning forward to access the landing ramp.

Floria was already out of her chair and running to the exit. Obi-Wan pushed Anakin ahead of him and they hurried after her, leaving the bomb behind.

As they raced down the ramp, Obi-Wan caught a glimpse of a figure dressed in black at the cargo door. He was trying to sneak aboard.

Floria screamed, and the bomb went off. Obi-Wan was blown off his feet. The figure in black went flying as well. Smoke rolled over them. Obi-Wan raised his head, trying to see. Coughing against the acrid smoke in his mouth, he struggled to his knees.

Obi-Wan peered through the rolling smoke to make sure Anakin and Floria were all right. Anakin was already standing and bending down to help a coughing Floria to rise.

"Anakin, check the area!" Obi-Wan shouted as he headed for the figure in black.

The figure rose shakily. Stumbling and falling, he attempted to run away. Obi-Wan raced toward him.

He had almost reached him when he felt something heavy land on his back. Hands covered his eyes. Hair brushed against his face.

Obi-Wan tried to twist away. "Floria?"

Suddenly the young slender girl had the moves of an assassin. She used a variety of intricate holds to slow down Obi-Wan while he struggled to move toward the figure in black. He tried to shake her off, but he didn't want to harm her.

Hands covered his eyes, and he carefully pried them off.

"I don't want to hurt you. . . ." he said.

She didn't answer, just wound one leg around his, trying to trip him, while she grabbed his ear.

"That's enough." Obi-Wan grabbed her wrists and

expertly flipped her over and down onto the ground. Her breath left her as she landed hard.

The figure in black hesitated. It was easy for Obi-Wan to stride forward and grab him by the scruff of the neck.

"All right, you two. What's going on?" he asked sternly.

Anakin ran back to him. "The blaster fire and explosions were set off by timed devices." He looked at Floria, who gazed up at Obi-Wan furiously from the ground. Then he looked at the squirming figure in Obi-Wan's grip. "What's going on?"

"That's what I'd like to know." Obi-Wan threw back the figure's black hood. Close-cropped blond hair and wide eyes the same brilliant blue as Floria's met his. The boy was only a few years older than Floria.

Obi-Wan looked at Floria. "Your brother, I presume."

The boy shot Floria a look clearly intended to keep her silent. Obi-Wan sighed. "Anakin, check his pack."

Anakin picked up a small pack the boy had worn on his back. He opened it and went through it. "Just some basic survival gear. A tarp and some rations."

Obi-Wan gave the boy a little shake. "I'm losing patience."

"Dane, we've been double-crossed," Floria said, rising gingerly and rubbing her elbow. "Why shouldn't we tell them? I'm getting a bad feeling about this planet. There was a sleeper bomb aboard that ship! That's totally against the rules!"

Dane said nothing.

"What rules?" Anakin asked.

"Now we're stuck here with the Jedi with no way to get off the planet," Floria continued. "We destroyed that ship for nothing. You and your big ideas!"

"You destroyed your own ship?" Anakin asked in disbelief.

"Cooperation doesn't seem like such a bad idea, considering the circumstances," Floria said, still speaking to her brother.

Dane shrugged. "So things didn't work out. They could have."

"But they didn't," Floria said.

"But they could have," Dane shot back.

"Who *are* you two?" Obi-Wan asked angrily, his patience exhausted.

"Bounty hunters," Floria said.

Anakin and Obi-Wan exchanged an incredulous look. These two young people, bounty hunters?

"Who are you hunting?" Anakin asked.

"You," Floria told him. "We're supposed to find the Jedi and bring you back, dead or alive."

"Bring us back where?" Obi-Wan asked. "Who hired you?"

"Let me just point out that we weren't going to kill you," Floria said quickly, not answering Obi-Wan's question. "We weren't the ones that planted the sleeper bomb, obviously."

"What about that blaster fire?" Anakin asked.

"We knew you could handle that. We just wanted to add a little urgency to the situation," Dane said. "You'd take off if you thought you were under attack."

"We didn't want to kill you," Floria assured them. "We don't kill beings. We just trick them. Just like we tricked you. It would have worked if there hadn't been that bomb. Listen, tricking is much safer."

"Are you actually successful at this?" Anakin asked.

Floria and Dane exchanged a look. Floria sighed. "Nobody ever believes we're bounty hunters. It's so insulting. Yes, we're successful. Take our last case. We —"

"Who hired you?" Obi-Wan asked in frustration, interrupting her brusquely.

"If you're going to confess everything, you might try to be organized about it," Dane said to Floria. "You always get off the subject."

"I don't," Floria protested.

"You do, too. Always."

"You shouldn't say always," Anakin broke in. "Absolutes are rarely true."

"Enough!" Obi-Wan roared. "Who hired you? I want answers, and I want them now."

Obi-Wan's thunderous look cowed Floria and Dane.

"Granta Omega," Floria said. "Do you know him? He's on his ship, orbiting the planet. Our plan was to lure you onto your own ship and get you to pilot it to what you'd think was my rendezvous ship but was actually Omega's transport. Then we'd leave you there, collect the reward, and take off. Easy, right?"

"Obviously not, since you're standing here with us now," Obi-Wan said. "So who put the sleeper bomb on the ship?"

"I don't know," Floria admitted.

"It could be anyone," Dane said. "Omega hired four other bounty hunters besides us. The first one to succeed wins the prize — and it's an enormous fortune. The only rule is that the bounty hunters aren't allowed to harm one another."

"Obviously, someone broke the rules," Floria said disapprovingly. "I could have died aboard that ship."

"Not to mention us," Anakin said.

"What about the other Jedi?" Obi-Wan asked.

"He's not part of the deal," Dane said. "We're supposed to go after the Master–Padawan team. That was it."

"What information were you given about us?" Obi-Wan asked. "How did you know where to find us?"

"We knew you were on a training mission on Ragoon-6," Floria said. "That's all."

That's all? That's too much. Obi-Wan couldn't believe it. The training missions weren't secret. But Jedi did not speak of them to outsiders. Of course, there were those in the Senate who knew about them. And Senators, Obi-Wan knew too well, could be bribed.

"Tell me about the other bounty hunters," Obi-Wan said. "Do you know them?"

Dane nodded. "They are well known to those who know about these things. Teleq is one. We know him by reputation only. He's known for his cunning use of technology. Then there is Mol Arcasite. She is ruthless. She will take innocent lives to get what she wants. And she doesn't care if she brings her prey back dead. Most bounty hunters prefer to catch beings alive. It saves them a possible security arrest themselves. You never know who might be watching."

"Mol gives us all a bad name," Floria said. "Come to think of it, she could have planted that sleeper bomb. It's just her style."

"What about the bounty hunter with the Stokhli stick?" Obi-Wan asked.

"Don't know him," Floria said. "He was awfully good. But he almost blew my cover when he saw me. I couldn't believe it when he said 'They were mine.'"

"So he was talking about us," Anakin said, indicating himself and Obi-Wan. "And you made us think you were concerned about your friends!"

Floria's eyes shone. "Wasn't I good?"

"She can cry on cue," Dane confided.

"Who is the last bounty hunter?" Obi-Wan asked.

"Hunti Pereg," Dane answered. "He has the most awesome reputation of all. He has never failed to capture his prey. Not once."

"Of course, he has never met the Jedi," Floria rushed to assure them.

Obi-Wan gave her an exasperated look. "Neither have you. If you had, you'd know we can see through flattery. You think Hunti Pereg can catch us."

"Well, he is very good," Floria said.

Obi-Wan stood, thinking a moment. Now he knew that those vague feelings had a source, after all. He knew one thing for sure: Wren had not left those clues. One of the bounty hunters had.

It was time to contact the Temple. A Jedi was in danger. He could feel it. But their comlinks had been blown up with the ship.

"We were deliberately led into that malia den," he told Anakin. "And the cavern. Someone left those clues for us to follow."

"Which means that Wren . . ." Anakin began.

"Has been captured or possibly even killed," Obi-Wan finished gravely. "But why? Why is this Granta Omega after us? What else do you know about him?"

"Not much. We've never seen him. We've communicated through comm channels. The only thing we know is that he is the richest being in the galaxy," Floria said.

"Not *the* richest," Dane corrected. "You always exaggerate."

"Okay, *one* of the richest," Floria said.

"Why has he targeted the Jedi?" Anakin asked.

Floria and Dane shook their heads. "We don't know," Floria said. "In this business, you don't ask too many questions. It's better not to get too involved."

"Speaking of which, hanging around with you two might be dangerous to our health," Dane said. "So if you don't mind, Floria and I will take our chances on Ragoon." He grabbed Floria's hand and began to edge away.

Obi-Wan blocked their path. "Not a chance," he said firmly. "You're not going anywhere until we find out exactly what's going on. We might need your help."

"What help could we possibly be?" Floria asked. "We told you everything we know."

"I'm sure you did not," Obi-Wan said. "You know the bounty hunters who are after us. You're not going anywhere until we know more about who is after us . . . and why."

CHAPTER NINE

"So, what now?" Anakin asked Obi-Wan.

"When you are the hunted, the best thing to do is to turn the tables," Obi-Wan said. "You must become the hunter."

"Track the bounty hunters," Anakin said.

Obi-Wan nodded. "We can start with the sleeper bomb. It needed a nearby power source to gather sufficient charge for someone to set it off. We need to find the power source, which won't be far."

"Whoa, wait a second," Floria said. "I didn't sign on for this. If you're going to chase down the rest of the bounty hunters, you've got to let us go. This could be dangerous."

"Bounty hunting isn't dangerous?" Anakin asked.

"We minimize our risks," Dane said. He hooked his

fingers into his thick black utility belt. "Which doesn't seem to be a consideration for Jedi."

"When it comes down to it, we just aren't very brave," Floria confessed.

"Speak for yourself, Floria," Dane said, scowling.

Floria ignored him. "So it's in your best interests to let us go. I tend to scream when trouble happens. And after all, it isn't fair. Bounty hunters are chasing you, not us. Why put us in harm's way?"

"Let me ask you something," Obi-Wan said. "Don't you think the bounty hunter knew you were aboard our ship before activating the signal?"

Floria bit her lip. "You mean we're a target, too?"

Obi-Wan shrugged. "Think about it. After all, the fewer bounty hunters there are, the easier it is to win the prize."

"But there are rules!" Floria protested. "Bounty hunters are forbidden to attack one another."

"In my experience, the larger the reward, the greater the chance rules will be broken," Obi-Wan said.

"Granta Omega wouldn't stand for it," Floria said, but she sounded less certain.

"Would you bet your life on the ethics of a being who is using bounty hunters to trap Jedi on a training exercise?" Obi-Wan asked mildly.

Floria was silent.

Obi-Wan waited while the sister and brother exchanged a glance. He was not about to let Floria and Dane go. Despite their assurances that they weren't dangerous, the reward would still tempt them to make trouble for the Jedi. Obi-Wan had no doubt that he and Anakin could handle any attack the bounty-hunting team could launch at them, but he'd rather not have to deal with it at all so he could focus on rescuing Wren and getting to the bottom of who was behind this.

He wanted them close. But it was better that they think it was in their best interests to stay with the Jedi.

"I think you've got us there," Dane told him. "Lead on."

With Floria and Dane in tow, Obi-Wan and Anakin began a systematic search. They walked outward from their ship in widening circles.

"The power source for that size sleeper bomb has to be a generator that's fairly large," Obi-Wan said. "I'm guessing it's on a cruiser of some kind."

"If the power source is on a cruiser, the bounty hunter could be long gone," Floria called to them as she brought up the rear.

"Not if the prize is as big as you say," Obi-Wan answered.

Their route took them over a rocky hill and down into another low-lying meadow. The ground was mushy beneath their feet. Ahead lay a boggy field full of shoulder-high bushes with bright yellow flowers.

Floria reached out to pick one. "Ow!" She sucked her finger.

Now they could see that red thorns surrounded the bright flowers.

"I guess we have to turn back," Floria said hopefully. "We'll be torn to shreds if we try to make it through these bushes."

Obi-Wan hesitated. Floria was right. But their only chance of finding the power source lay in examining the surrounding area.

"Master," Anakin said quietly.

Obi-Wan heard it, too. The faint whine of a cruiser engine. He searched the sky and saw nothing.

"Everyone get down low," he said.

They crouched underneath the bushes in a hollowed-out spot while Obi-Wan and Anakin scanned the sky.

The cruiser darted into view, a flash of silver against the blue.

"Fast, agile," Anakin reported, squinting at it. "Laser cannons mounted on either side of the bridge."

"It's Mol Arcasite's cruiser," Dane said. "I recognize

it. She had it techno-tweaked by Sienar's Advanced Projects. Uh-oh."

The cruiser had made a sharp turn and now headed straight toward them.

Dane looked around. "What are we going to do? There's no place to hide. And if we go back we'll be caught in the open."

Obi-Wan withdrew his lightsaber and activated it. He leaned forward and expertly sliced through the thorny bush. The bush melted away.

"Those things sure come in handy," Floria said admiringly.

The cruiser darted lower. The laser cannons suddenly burst into a clatter of rapid fire.

"Move!" Obi-Wan urged as the fire scorched the bushes behind them. He darted through the hole he'd created with his lightsaber, swinging it in a short arc in order to clear the way farther into the brush.

Anakin pushed Floria through and waited for Dane to dart in before following. Obi-Wan used the lightsaber with a fine-honed precision, cutting a hole in the bush just below the surface so that the bushes would seem intact from the air. There would be no telltale path to advertise their progress.

Obi-Wan moved fast, but in a wide zigzag over the

length of the field. They grew tired and sweaty and were scratched by the long, sharp thorns. Still, Obi-Wan pushed on, making Mol Arcasite dive again and again over the thorny field. At times the cannon fire was so close Obi-Wan could feel the heat from the blaster bolts.

"Is this a plan?" Dane asked. A long scratch went from his ear to his nose. "Because it doesn't seem like a plan. Are you trying to tire out a cruiser?"

Obi-Wan didn't answer. He had brought them to the edge of the field. Ahead was another rocky hill, the beginning of the foothills to the mountains.

"Stay here," Obi-Wan told Floria and Dane. "Anakin, follow me."

He stepped out into the open. He held his lightsaber high.

"She's had to fly low and buzz us continually," he told Anakin. "I see some slight smoke from the forward laser cannon."

"She could be overheating," Anakin said. "That's why you kept her moving."

"Exactly. Now let's keep going."

It was a challenge, but the Jedi moved fast, using the natural formation of the steep hill and the surrounding boulders for cover. Again and again, Mol Arcasite dived toward them, laser cannons blasting, but they used the deep rocky overhangs for cover.

"I'm going to try something," Obi-Wan told Anakin. "Keep her occupied down here."

As soon as the cruiser banked and turned for another approach, Obi-Wan leaped up to an overhang, then jumped to the next, and the next. Now he was above the low-flying cruiser, which was angling in to attack Anakin.

Obi-Wan activated his lightsaber. The bright blue glow attracted Mol Arcasite's attention. She reversed course and came at him, cannons blazing. Obi-Wan leaped toward the ground, bypassing the ledges he'd used to climb up. Cannon fire shattered the rock as the cruiser dived to follow him. An avalanche of rocks rained down on the body of the cruiser.

Obi-Wan landed lightly next to Anakin. "Good work, Master," Anakin said, watching the cruiser. "More smoke coming from that left side. That cannon might overheat."

"Good. Now for the final blow. Follow me." Obi-Wan jumped back up the hill. Anakin followed, moving from ledge to ledge until they had reached the top. Below them, shadows cast by an overhang concealed a thick fall of snow. In the shelter of the rock, the snow had not melted with the morning sun.

"When the cruiser returns, activate your cable launcher and jump," Obi-Wan told Anakin.

Anakin nodded, guessing his Master's plan.

"If it doesn't work, we'll be hanging there, perfect targets," Obi-Wan said. "So keep a free hand for your lightsaber." He kept his eyes on the cruiser. "Ready — go!"

The Master and Padawan swung off the mountain on their cable launchers. The sudden move caught Mol Arcasite by surprise. The cruiser dived after them, firing rapidly.

The noise and heat of the blaster bolts released an avalanche of snow and chunks of ice. The large blanket fell directly on the cruiser, blinding Mol Arcasite momentarily. Obi-Wan and Anakin hung on to their cable launchers as the snow showered down past them. The cruiser wobbled crazily, heading straight for the stone side of the mountain.

At the last moment before the cruiser hit, a cargo door opened and a swoop zoomed out. They could see that Mol Arcasite was astride it.

The cruiser crashed into the mountain with a whoosh and roar of fuel. Obi-Wan and Anakin kept under the shelter of a ledge as flaming metal rained down below.

The swoop took off into the distance, became a black speck, and disappeared.

Obi-Wan and Anakin lowered themselves to the ground. Floria and Dane rushed toward them.

"That was incredible," Floria said. "You defeated Mol Arcasite! I'm not betting on Hunti Pereg anymore."

"You're rid of Mol Arcasite for good," Dane told them. "She's good, but she's known for not sticking around if her first strike fails badly. She just lost a ship. Her own survival is her first priority."

"That doesn't sound like good business for a bounty hunter," Anakin said.

"She seldom fails," Dane said. "So it doesn't matter. No doubt she has a backup plan. She'll be onto her next assignment by nightfall."

"So we've got one paralyzed bounty hunter, and another one took off," Obi-Wan said. "That leaves two."

"So what next?" Dane asked. Now he looked interested in the Jedi's strategy.

"We know that Wren didn't leave the clues for us to follow," Obi-Wan said. "The question is, who did?"

"I'm betting on Teleq," Dane said. "It's just his style. He's clever, and he's fond of traps."

"Whoever it is doesn't know that we know we're being hunted," Obi-Wan pointed out. "As a matter of fact, he's probably still leaving clues for us to follow."

"So what should we do?" Floria leaned forward eagerly.

Obi-Wan noted her eagerness. Now Floria was on

their side. Or else she was hoping that once the Jedi eliminated all the other bounty hunters, she and Dane would find a way to take the prize.

One way or another, it didn't matter. He wanted to keep Floria and Dane close.

"We give him exactly what he wants. We follow them, of course," Obi-Wan said.

CHAPTER TEN

Obi-Wan and Anakin retraced their steps, climbing the mountain again. Floria and Dane trudged behind them, unused to the quick pace the Jedi set.

"I'm beginning to think I'd rather take my chances with the bounty hunters," Floria grumbled.

Anakin stopped in order to fall into place next to her. "How did you and Dane get into this line of work?" he asked. "Where are your parents?"

"Where are yours?" Floria snapped. Suddenly her face shut down and became defensive and angry.

"My mother lives on Tatooine," Anakin said. "She is a slave."

Floria's face softened slightly. "Oh. I'm sorry. Our parents are dead. I don't come from Aaeton. That was a lie. Dane and I are from the Inner Core world of Thracior. We grew up in peaceful times, but five years ago the warlords of Thracior began to argue over territory. Raids began between the different tribes. My mother was a Hnsi, my father a Tantt. They were killed because they intermarried. The Hnsis burned our house down and killed our baby sister. Dane and I escaped."

Floria told the story in a monotone, her eyes on the mountain trail. Ahead of them, Dane did not turn or acknowledge he was listening, but Anakin saw his neck flush red.

"Dane and I had to make our way as best we could," Floria said. "We had lost everything, so we had to work. We found jobs in a café at a space station, washing up and serving food. Our boss was a very cruel man. We discovered he was wanted by the security forces of a nearby planet. We tricked him into getting caught. We got the reward, but we had to leave the planet. So we kind of fell into bounty hunting. We've been moving around the galaxy ever since."

"When you find something you're good at, you stick with it," Dane said with a cocky assurance Anakin did not quite believe.

"It sounds like a hard life," Anakin remarked.

Floria cocked an eyebrow. "And is yours so easy, Jedi?"

Anakin took the question seriously. "In a way, it is,"

he said slowly. "I know I am being of service. That makes the path easy to walk."

"Well, I'd rather go down my path in a nice, techno-maxed cruiser," Floria said. "So I guess I'm stuck with bounty hunting."

"Here we are," Obi-Wan called from a short distance ahead. "We left the path here, when we thought some-one was following us."

"That was me," Floria said.

Obi-Wan nodded. "Let's find the next clue, Anakin."

Anakin left Floria's side. He pushed their conversa-tion out of his mind. Earlier, finding clues had been fun. Now, it would be serious.

It didn't take long to find the next clue. After a fork in the path, they found a few crumbs from a blumfruit muffin left near a flat rock alongside the trail.

"He is clever," Obi-Wan told Anakin, squatting by the clue. "He is leading us on without tipping us off. But we know that Wren would never have left this clue."

Anakin briefly tasted the crumbs. He looked up at his Master, his face grave. "These are from the Temple."

"Are you sure?" Obi-Wan asked.

Anakin nodded. "I'd know Jedi Knight Alicka's muffins anywhere. This must mean that —"

"The bounty hunter definitely has Wren. He has raided his survival pack."

They hurried on. They had lost a good deal of time, and Anakin could tell that his Master was worried about Wren's fate.

They followed the path until it curved along a ridge that overlooked a meadow full of tall, slender, flowering trees. From above, the flowering branches formed a solid carpet of pink. Anakin stopped and examined a large boulder on the side of the trail. He hopped from one boulder to the next.

"This way," he called to Obi-Wan. "He went down from here to the meadow."

He looked back up at his Master. Obi-Wan's gaze swept the trees below. "Wren is near. I can feel it. Let's proceed carefully."

They made their way carefully down the slope, jumping from rock to rock. Floria and Dane followed at a distance. When they reached the meadow, the perfume of the flowering trees hit their nostrils. Under any other circumstances, Anakin would have paused to drink in the beauty of the spot. After growing up on a desert world, he was often overwhelmed by simple things such as flowers and grasses.

The trees had slender triangular trunks, but the branches were thick and wide. The flowers were so large and dense that the top of each tree was a waving mass of frothy pink.

Anakin scanned the meadow, alert for trouble. But instead, he saw Wren sleeping under a tree.

"Master —"

"I see him." Obi-Wan paused. "Something is . . . not right," he murmured. "I get no sense of the Force from Wren."

Anakin frowned. His Master was right.

Obi-Wan took a step forward. But it was not in the direction Anakin had been looking.

"Master?"

Anakin saw that his Master had headed toward Wren. But this was a different Wren, sleeping under a different tree.

And then Anakin saw another Wren, and another, and another. None of them was the real Jedi. They were merely projections of his image.

"Holograms," Obi-Wan said.

"All of them?" Anakin asked.

He looked at his Master. There was no way to know.

CHAPTER ELEVEN

"Stay here and don't try anything," Obi-Wan warned Floria and Dane. "We will handle this."

"Be my guest," Dane answered, his eyes darting to the many Wrens.

"Teleq wants us to run into the meadow," Obi-Wan murmured to Anakin. "He wants us to race from one image of Wren to another. So we won't."

They didn't need to. They would use the Force.

Obi-Wan and Anakin reached out and gathered it around them. A fellow Jedi was in danger. That made their connection to the Force even stronger, made their ability to gather it more urgent.

Obi-Wan felt the power of Anakin's grasp of the Force. As always, it staggered him.

He scanned the meadow once more, and this time

he knew which of the images was not an image. Which one was Wren. When he looked directly at Wren, he felt the answering surge. Anakin had also honed in on the real Wren.

The sound of Obi-Wan's lightsaber leaving his belt was no more than a whisper. His leaving his spot was no more than a disturbance of the air. Yet he was gone, across the meadow, racing toward Wren. He could feel rather than hear Anakin behind him.

Suddenly, Wren's body snapped into the air. Obi-Wan watched, his heart in his mouth, as Wren was hoisted up into the trees. There was no question in Obi-Wan's mind that Wren must have been given a paralyzing drug of some kind. He could tell by the boneless way Wren's legs and arms flopped as if he were a puppet.

Rage bloomed in his chest. Obi-Wan absorbed it and let it go. He did not need rage to fight this. He needed discipline. Calm.

He anticipated the attack before it came. He had known Teleq was luring them on, but he did not care. He was ready to meet the bounty hunter.

He had just not expected the attack to come from above. A shower of poisonous darts rained down from the trees.

"Flechette canisters," Obi-Wan told Anakin. He shifted his focus to the branches over his head. Now he could see Teleq. He was a long-limbed being with hooked fingers and toes, making him adept at climbing and swinging through the trees.

Perched on the branches were also flocks of birds. Their feathers were the same bright pink as the flowering trees, allowing them to blend into their surroundings. They were almost as big as Anakin, with large wings folded back against their bodies.

As Teleq moved from branch to branch, the birds began to squawk angrily. Obi-Wan leaped to catch a branch high overhead, then swung himself up into the trees. A bird pecked his hand, drawing blood. He swung up to the next branch. The tree was easy to climb, since the branches were wide and flat. He could see Teleq trying to scamper away, firing another shower of darts at him over his shoulder.

Anakin swung himself into a tree close by. He climbed up onto another branch, then another. High above the ground the branches were close together, and they would be able to leap from one tree to another to pursue Teleq.

But where was Teleq headed? Obi-Wan wondered as he climbed. He watched Teleq jump to another tree and realized what he was doing.

Teleq was leading them closer to Wren. The closer Obi-Wan got to Teleq, the more he would bring Wren into the range of fire of the darts. And Wren would be unable to deflect them.

What is his objective? Obi-Wan wondered. How was he planning to catch the Jedi?

The possibilities flew through Obi-Wan's mind, presenting themselves so quickly it was as though they appeared all at once.

Wren himself is booby-trapped.

There is another trap in Wren's tree.

There is a trap on the logical progression to Wren's tree.

There is no trap. Teleq is planning a surprise move with the flechette canister or another weapon.

The question is, how can I surprise him instead?

Anakin leaped from his tree to the next one, deflecting a shower of darts with a series of quick lightsaber moves. Obi-Wan leaped to another tree, still considering his options. Suddenly his mind cleared, leaving a space without sound. He knew what would follow: Qui-Gon's voice. Often, it arose in his mind just when he was most confused or uncertain.

Use everything you have. Use the ground. Use the sky. Use what is around you.

Another bird suddenly squawked by his ear. Obi-Wan deftly moved to the left as the bird struck out with a long, pointed beak. Another bird leaped closer on the thick branch, screeching at Obi-Wan. He realized that he had almost stumbled into a nest. No wonder the birds were so furious. He quickly jumped to the branch of the next tree.

He didn't like the setting of this battle. Teleq was adept at navigating the trees. He had chosen his ground wisely. And Obi-Wan couldn't help the nagging suspicion that somehow Teleq was luring them into a trap. They would have to get him first. But how?

Another bird squawked overhead, its mate joining it to circle above a nest.

Use everything you have . . .

While he deflected more darts from the flechette canister, Obi-Wan searched the branches near Wren's tree. Obviously, Teleq was trying to drive them there. He was being clever about it — he was trying to make them think that he was attempting to keep them away from the tree — but Obi-Wan knew better.

There — he saw it. A large nest near Teleq, guarded by two birds. That would do.

He did not have time to communicate his plan to Anakin. He would have to trust that his Padawan would get the idea.

Obi-Wan jumped from his tree to the next, and the next, following the route he felt sure Teleq wanted him to follow. He kept his lightsaber activated, swinging at the darts to clear his way. He could hear Anakin behind him, jumping from tree to tree.

When they were closer to Teleq, Obi-Wan swung off to another tree to his right. Anakin hesitated, then moved in the opposite direction.

It was not the first time that Obi-Wan was grateful for his Padawan's excellent instincts. Time and again, Anakin would read Obi-Wan's strategy faster than Obi-Wan ever expected.

Moving fast now, the two Jedi leaped from tree branch to tree branch. Obi-Wan could not see Teleq's face, but he could tell by his movements and the frantic bursts from the flechette canister that the bounty hunter was unnerved.

As Obi-Wan grew closer, Anakin swung out to the side, so that Teleq was forced to move back, exactly where Obi-Wan wanted him.

Obi-Wan gathered the Force. It would be a difficult leap, bypassing one tree to land on another. But it was the only way to surprise Teleq enough to get him to leap to the next tree.

Obi-Wan jumped. The speed and power of the move surprised Teleq. Obi-Wan saw the shock on his face as he stumbled on the wide branch, then awkwardly leaped to the next tree. At the same time, Obi-Wan changed direction in midair. He collided with Teleq, sending the bounty hunter sailing straight into a bird's nest.

Screeee! Screeeee! Screeee! Screeee! The birds erupted in wild, furious calls. Two small baby birds lifted their heads and tried to flap their wings at the intruder.

The two large birds guarding the nest suddenly rose in the air. Together, they extended their powerful claws and snatched Teleq from the nest. Beating their wings, they carried a struggling Teleq away.

Anakin leaped onto the branch next to Obi-Wan. "Good plan, Master."

"We need to get Wren down from that tree. It can't be as easy as it looks." Obi-Wan leaped from branch to branch. When he got onto the tree next to Wren's, he examined the area carefully. Wren could not move his eyes, yet Obi-Wan felt the Force roll out from him in strong waves. Wren was warning him.

"I know, Wren," he called to him. "We will take our time, but we'll get you out."

The ground at the bottom of the tree was thickly carpeted with blooms, just like every other tree. But here the blooms were massed a little too thickly. The pattern was not random enough.

"Anakin, swing down and examine the ground under

the tree," Obi-Wan instructed. "But be careful. Don't get too close."

Anakin eased down to the ground. He circled the tree, gazing carefully down. "These blossoms have been placed here."

"That's what I thought."

"Something is underneath." Before Obi-Wan could stop him, Anakin tossed a rock into the mass of flowers. It disappeared.

"There's a trench down there," Anakin called up.

"You're lucky there wasn't an explosive," Obi-Wan said disapprovingly. Sometimes Anakin acted too rashly. If he could teach the boy one thing, it would be to wait.

He began to study the tree branches. He noticed seams running through several of the branches.

"I think I get it," he called down to Anakin. "These branches have been cut through, then resealed. They won't take our weight. We would have crashed through, right into that trench."

"And then he could have hit us with some paralyzing darts," Anakin finished. "Pretty simple plan."

"Simple is sometimes best," Obi-Wan said. "Lucky for us, it was not in this case. We'll have to use our cable launchers to get Wren."

Activating their launchers, the Jedi swung close to

Wren and managed to cut him free. Obi-Wan supported him as he released his cable launcher and they dropped to the ground.

He carefully lay Wren down and examined him. There was a long gash on one leg and his arm looked bruised. He had a blaster wound to the shoulder. He must have been in pain.

Obi-Wan reached for the bacta in his kit and administered it.

"You will be fine, but you need better care than we can give you here," he told Wren. "We must get you back to the Temple."

"That means we need a ship," Anakin said.

"Teleq's must be nearby," Obi-Wan said, rising to his feet.

Anakin looked around. "Where are Floria and Dane? They were supposed to wait by the hill."

"I think I know where I can find them, too," Obi-Wan said.

CHAPTER TWELVE

Floria and Dane sat by Teleq's ship at the end of the meadow. They jumped up when they saw Obi-Wan and Anakin.

"We saw the battle," Floria said. "I'll never underestimate the Jedi again. The way you strategized! The way you moved!"

"Nice star cruiser," Anakin said, circling around Teleq's ship. "We could get to Coruscant on this."

"Don't bother going inside yet," Obi-Wan said. "The engine's been disabled."

Anakin poked his head around the side of the ship and looked at Obi-Wan quizzically. Obi-Wan looked at Floria and Dane.

"Well?" he said sternly.

Dane opened his hand. A sensor lay in it. "Just a little part," he said. "And the engine is easily fixed. It's an activation sensor for the sublight drive."

"So Teleq wouldn't be able to leave the atmosphere," Anakin said. "He'd have to rely on repulsorlift engines."

"And a warning light would tell him so," Obi-Wan finished. "He'd know he wouldn't be able to take off without work on the engine. And while he was working on it, you'd disable *him*. And take off with us for the prize."

Floria tried to smile. "Hey, it was worth a try."

"Wait a second," Anakin said. "This means that you expected Teleq to capture us!"

"No offense," Dane said. "What kind of bounty hunters would we be if we didn't explore all the alternatives?"

Glaring at Dane, Anakin strode forward and snatched the part from his hand. "Don't worry, Master. I can fix the engine in no time at all."

Anakin accessed the engine panel on the exterior of the ship. He withdrew a small hydrospanner from his utility kit and his head disappeared inside. Muffled exclamations floated out to the others.

Finally Anakin emerged, his face streaked with grease. "You shorted out the sublight engine fuses and deactivated the power converter! I can't fix this!"

"I did?" Dane looked surprised. "I didn't mean to. I

don't know that much about engines," he confided to Obi-Wan.

Floria smacked her brother on the arm. "I told you to be careful! Now how are we supposed to get out of here?"

"You're the one who told me to disable it!" Dane protested.

"You said it was a good idea! If I'd known you didn't know how, I wouldn't have suggested it!"

Obi-Wan heaved an exasperated breath. If he could leave these two behind, he would. But something told him that he still needed them. "Stop squabbling, you two. We have to take Wren back to the Temple. We'll have to return and find the other bounty hunter's ship."

"Go back down the mountain?" Floria asked in dismay. "I'm exhausted!"

"And dusk will be here soon," Dane added.

Obi-Wan shouldered his pack. "Then we'd better get started."

They left Wren wrapped in a blanket inside Teleq's ship. Anakin was able to reconfigure the ship's security code so that Wren would be protected inside. Even if Teleq somehow managed to get free of those birds, he would not be able to board his ship. At least Wren would have warmth and shelter. Promising to return soon, they set off down the mountain again.

"It's been almost five hours," Obi-Wan told Anakin. "With luck, the bounty hunter will be just getting over his paralysis. He'll have no choice but to cooperate."

"We certainly are developing a collection of bounty hunters," Anakin remarked.

"Unfortunately they're not all as harmless as Floria and Dane," Obi-Wan said.

Anakin looked at him curiously. "You knew Floria wasn't telling the truth from the beginning, didn't you?"

"I suspected as much," Obi-Wan admitted. "But I had no way of knowing what she was concealing."

"I believed her story," Anakin said, frowning. "Why didn't the Force warn me?"

Obi-Wan smiled. "The Force is not a truth serum, Padawan. The ability to read a being's true motives comes with experience and patience. I was once very bad at it. Qui-Gon taught me how to look and listen. Floria betrayed herself by playing on our sympathies just a bit too much."

"And you knew they would find Teleq's ship and try to disable it."

"Experience," Obi-Wan said. "It tells me that beings follow their best interests. Floria and Dane have had to fight their way through the galaxy. They are used to looking out for themselves. Naturally they would still try to foil another bounty hunter winning the prize."

Obi-Wan put a hand on Anakin's shoulder. "Do not trouble yourself, Padawan. You have an open heart. This is a good thing. With time you will learn the balance you need in a galaxy where all beings do not tell the truth. Your impulsiveness is a source of energy and power for you. But it can lead to trouble. You will learn to be more careful. Sometimes it is better to walk than run."

"I got us into trouble with the malia, and then in the cavern," Anakin admitted. "I am sorry, Master."

"Danger finds us on every mission," Obi-Wan said. "Let us look forward."

They followed the winding path down the mountain once again. When they reached the site of their battle with the Tursha, they hurried through the meadow. Ahead they could see the camouflaged tent. As they walked forward, they could distinguish the Tursha still slumped against the tree.

"He's still paralyzed," Anakin said, starting forward.

Obi-Wan stopped him. "No, Padawan. He is dead."

CHAPTER THIRTEEN

Obi-Wan crouched over the body. "Poisoned," he said.

Anakin leaned forward curiously. "Flechette canister?"

"No. See the flecks on his lips? It was a fast poison, injected in the neck." Obi-Wan gently moved the Tursha's head. "Here." Obi-Wan stood. "Do you have your tarp?"

Anakin withdrew the tarp from his survival pack. Gently, Obi-Wan wrapped the body. "We will come back for him," he murmured. "We must take him to Coruscant. He might have had family." He stood, his eyes roaming the area. "Now we must return to our problem. We must find his ship."

They split up and searched the area thoroughly, but they could not find the ship the bounty hunter had used.

"One of the other bounty hunters must have stolen it," Obi-Wan said. "Mol Arcasite, perhaps."

"Do you think she killed him?"

"Possibly," Obi-Wan said. "But one of the others could have done it. We have no way to know."

"What now?" Anakin wondered. "We're stuck on the planet with no comm unit."

"We have one last sabaac card to play," Obi-Wan said. He turned to Floria and Dane.

"What?" Floria shifted nervously. "We told you everything we know."

"I don't think so," Obi-Wan answered. "If you had captured us, where would you have taken us?"

"To Granta Omega, of course," Dane answered.

"How would you have contacted him?" Obi-Wan asked. "You must have some sort of prearranged line of communication."

Floria and Dane gave each other a nervous look.

"Because you're going to use it. You're going to contact him and tell him that you've captured us," Obi-Wan said. "And you're going to ask him to meet you on Ragoon-6."

"What if we do?" Floria asked. "Do you think we're crazy enough to contact Granta Omega and lie to him?"

Obi-Wan merely looked at them. It was enough.

"All right, all right," Floria muttered. "We'll contact

Granta Omega and lie to him. Just arrange a really nice funeral for us, will you?"

Obi-Wan shook his head. "No funerals. But the game is over. We're not chasing any more bounty hunters. Granta Omega will come to us."

Floria agreed grudgingly. "I guess we'll cooperate. I'm tired of trying to outthink you, anyway. Obviously, we're outmatched. Besides, I'm starting to like you. And I bet Dane is, too."

Dane groaned. "Guilty. Some bounty hunters we are. We befriend our prey instead of betraying them. Okay." He gazed seriously at Obi-Wan. "If we do this, will you protect us?"

Obi-Wan nodded. "You have my word."

Slowly, Dane withdrew a comlink from a hidden pocket in his cloak. "It's only got one channel," he said. "It's a direct line to Omega." Dane activated it and inputted a code.

"We have the Jedi," he said. "But we lost our transport. You must come to us."

He listened for a moment, then shut off the comlink. "He's agreed to meet us. He sounded surprised that Floria and I were the ones to catch you. Kind of insulting, actually. But he's coming." Dane looked at his sister. "Unfortunately, he wants to meet us on top of the mountain."

Floria groaned. "Not again."

"Don't worry," Obi-Wan said. "We'll get up a faster way."

This time, they did not follow the trail. They used cable launchers to vault straight up the cliffs. From that spot, they were able to hike above the tree line. The air was thin and cold here, and Obi-Wan and Anakin paused to don their thermal capes. The snow was ankle-deep on the trail.

"There's a good chance he'll be wary," Obi-Wan told Anakin. "We must pretend to be Dane and Floria's prisoners until the last possible moment. I don't have to tell you that we need to take Granta Omega alive. Perhaps more important than catching him will be finding out why and how he targeted us."

Floria and Dane slipped laser cuffs over Anakin and Obi-Wan's wrists but did not seal them. It would appear that the two were prisoners. They marched ahead of Floria and Dane.

"Wasn't it your idea to become bounty hunters?" Floria grumbled to her brother as she pushed her way through the snow. "'Floria, we can see the galaxy. Floria, it will be fun. Floria, it's an easy way to make a fortune —'"

"Floria, you're driving me crazy," Dane interrupted.

"We're getting closer, you two," Obi-Wan warned

from behind them. "Try to act like professionals. We could be under surveillance."

"Master, there is someone ahead," Anakin said under his breath.

A humanoid male sat on top of ice-encrusted snow ahead. He was dressed all in white, and had blended in with the snow.

"It must be Hunti Pereg," Dane murmured to them. "He's the only bounty hunter left."

The stranger did not move as they approached.

"Greetings," Dane called. "We are Dane and Floria, bounty hunters. We have caught the Jedi."

The man smiled pleasantly. "I can see that. Congratulations. I am Hunti Pereg. Bounty hunter as well."

Obi-Wan was poised for an assault. Surely the fearsome Hunti Pereg would not let two children take away his prize. His face looked fierce and frightening. It had the patched-together look of a recent application of synth-flesh, as though he had been badly injured.

The scars of the life of a bounty hunter, Obi-Wan thought. It bothered him to think of young Floria and Dane continuing with such a life. Despite their grumbles and their tricks, they were not bad creatures.

And they are exactly the sort of beings Qui-Gon would befriend. And I would not understand why. Now I do, Qui-Gon. Now, I do.

"Don't worry, kids," Pereg told them. "I won't inter-
fere with your prize."

"I'm glad to see you abide by the rules of honor,"
Dane said.

"It's not that," Pereg said. "I can't move my legs.
That scoundrel son of a gravel-maggot Teleq shot me
with a paralyzing dart four hours ago. So it looks like
you've won."

"Is there anything we can do for you?" Floria asked
politely. "It's awfully cold up here."

"Very kind of you to ask," Pereg said. "After you collect the reward, if you wouldn't mind sending a ship
back for me, I'd appreciate it. Professional courtesy. I'll
make it worth your while."

"Have you seen Granta Omega, by any chance?"
Floria asked him.

He shook his head. "Sorry. It's just been me and
the mountain."

They left Hunti Pereg behind and continued to the
rendezvous point. They were almost at the top of the
mountain now. The sun had slid behind the peak, and
the wind had picked up. A few snowflakes drifted down
from a white sky. Floria wrapped her cloak tighter
around her.

They stopped at the coordinates Granta had given
them. They looked up at the sky, waiting to see a ship.

Dane got out a tarp with thermal coils and spread it on the ground. He and Floria sat, trying to keep warm. Obi-Wan and Anakin stood, holding their arms so the laser cuffs were visible. Obi-Wan did not feel the cold.

The minutes ticked by.

"He isn't coming," Obi-Wan said at last.

"Do you think he knows it was a trick?" Anakin asked.

"There's no way to know," Obi-Wan said. "But a storm is coming, and we need to find help for Wren. We'll have to track Omega after we get Wren to safety."

"How?" Anakin asked. "We don't have a ship."

"We'll have to take another look at Teleq's," Obi-Wan decided.

Floria stood. "At last I can get off this mountain."

"Well, at least all the bounty hunters have been accounted for," Anakin said. "We don't have to worry about being attacked."

They started back down the trail, their footsteps crunching through the thin skin of ice into the densely packed snow.

Obi-Wan heard a slight whistling noise behind him. A small metal ball whizzed by his ear and caught the light as it arced through the air.

"Hit the ground!" Obi-Wan shouted as he vaulted forward and pulled Floria and Dane down underneath him.

CHAPTER FOURTEEN

The explosion sent a shower of snow high into the air. Obi-Wan lifted his head. The thermal detonator had hit thirty meters away. That was close. Detonators had a twenty-meter radius of destruction.

Three Attack Droids headed toward them, gliding just above the surface of the snow with repulsorlift engines.

There was no cover. They could not avoid this battle, even if they'd wanted to. They would have to protect Floria and Dane and foil their attacker. He or she was fighting wisely, attacking without advancing.

At this point, Obi-Wan was getting a little tired of bounty hunters.

Obi-Wan put his hand on Dane's back. "Stay down," he ordered him swiftly. "We will take care of this."

Dane nodded and covered Floria protectively with his own body.

Anakin's lightsaber blazed in his hand. Obi-Wan nodded and they raced toward the advancing droids, swinging their lightsabers to deflect the blaster bolts. They had to be careful. A stray bolt could hit Dane, who was out in the open.

Anakin leaped toward the first droid. He cut it down with one stroke. Blaster bolts melted the snow around him, but Anakin was already twisting in midair to get out of the way. He landed lightly in precisely the right spot to launch another attack.

He had factored in the icy skin on top of the snow, but his foot still slipped slightly. Anakin took a moment to get his balance. He had forgotten about the thermal detonators. Obi-Wan saw the two balls whizzing toward Anakin. There was no time for him to reach the spot. He reached down and scooped up two large rocks. He threw one with each hand. Each rock flew unerringly toward its target, hitting the thermal detonators in midair, causing them to veer off course. They sailed by on either side of Anakin's head and fell twenty-five meters away. Too close.

Obi-Wan charged forward. The remaining two droids were trying to outflank the Jedi. He fanned out and

Anakin did the same. Then they ran toward each other, each targeting a droid as they jumped, their lightsabers held high. The droids fell with a sizzle in two smoking piles into the snow.

Obi-Wan could see the attacker now. It was another bounty hunter. He was tall and lean and dressed in plastoid armor. Two harnesses were slung crosswise around his body, filled with a variety of weapons. Attached to his belt were more thermal detonators.

He flipped one toward the Jedi. Obi-Wan and Anakin could not deflect it with their lightsabers. They would not be able to get close enough. They had exactly six seconds to move out of the way.

Obi-Wan reached for the cable line on his belt. He lassoed the detonator and jerked the line, sending it in the opposite direction, back toward the attacker. He saw the attacker bare his teeth in an admiring smile at the Jedi's skill even as he reached up to catch it in his bare hand. Then he flung it backward, where it detonated harmlessly.

The attacker did not have to move. His weapons could be launched from a distance. But Obi-Wan and Anakin had to maneuver through deep snow to get to him. Anakin had his cable line out and was ready to lasso the next detonator. Obi-Wan ran through the snow. The wind had formed deep drifts, and he had to use the Force to guide him. He used his lightsaber to melt the snow when it piled up against him.

The detonators flew toward them furiously. Occasionally they could hit one with a rock, or lasso one with a cable line. But mostly the two Jedi had to outrun them.

Obi-Wan's legs were beginning to tire from struggling against the snow. He could hear the rasp of Anakin's breath. How long could they keep this up? Obi-Wan wondered.

Beside the attacker, Obi-Wan saw steam rising from the snow. He caught a glint of water and realized it was a thermal spring.

"Anakin, head right," he called to his Padawan.

They moved slightly to the attacker's right. Every time they moved, they brought him closer to the spring.

Ten detonators left on his belt. Obi-Wan took a chance and leaped, ducking to avoid a detonator headed his way. It exploded, and he felt the shock waves against his skin. He landed on the snow awkwardly and slid down the slope toward his attacker.

Anakin leaped in order to land in front of him, blocking his descent. Two detonators headed their way, and Obi-Wan lassoed one and sent it crashing into the other. The two smoking orbs fell into deep snow.

"The thermal pool," he said to Anakin. "Drive him toward it."

Anakin nodded. He looked tired. Obi-Wan was, too. Yet he knew that beyond their fatigue lay their stamina.

When they were close enough, Obi-Wan risked a leap straight at the attacker. He knew he would cause him to back up, and the attacker did. He slid on the ice and fell back, crashing into the spring.

The attacker slipped beneath the surface of the water, then emerged, treading water. He shook the hair out of his eyes and gazed at Obi-Wan with a hostile look.

Obi-Wan stood at the edge. He held out a hand. "You have about ten seconds."

"Yes."

The attacker knew the extreme heat would cause a fusion reaction. The thermal detonators would blow.

His eyes were a vivid color somewhere between silver and lilac. There was a scar on his upper lip. His hair was long and tied back with a silver cord.

"Come on," Obi-Wan said, keeping his hand steady. "We won't hurt you."

"Not you, but another," the bounty hunter said. "If I return to him without you, he will kill me anyway. I will have an easier death this way. You don't know his power. It comes from the pyramid itself."

"You don't have to return to him," Obi-Wan said.

"Ah. But he will find me." The bounty hunter closed his eyes.

Obi-Wan reached out over the water. "You must give up!"

"I cannot," the bounty hunter replied, his eyes still closed. "And I must tell you this — neither will he."

Obi-Wan leaped into the pool. But it was too late. The thermal detonators exploded. Water rose and hit Obi-Wan in the face. He choked and slipped beneath the water, then surfaced, struggling against the waves created by the explosion. Smoke rolled toward him.

The smoke cleared. Deep below the clear surface of the water, he saw the bounty hunter's body spiral down, down, to a bottomless pool beneath.

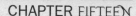

CHAPTER FIFTEEN

Anakin hurried over to the thermal pool. His Master had hauled himself out and stood at the edge. The steaming water pooled at his feet, melting the snow.

Through the smoke and steam, he could see the sadness on his Master's face. The Force was strong here. His Master was reaching out to it and gathering it around, as though warming himself. Obi-Wan's gaze was far away.

"Master? Are you all right?"

"I am saying good-bye to a being I did not know," Obi-Wan said softly.

The reverence in his tone surprised Anakin. "He could have killed you."

"Yet he did not. There is always a need for grief when a being dies, Padawan. Qui-Gon taught me that."

Obi-Wan looked down into the steaming pool. "I saw someone take his own life in a pool like this one. It was Xanatos, Qui-Gon's greatest enemy. A being who hated Qui-Gon and who would stop at nothing to destroy him. Still, when he took his own life, Qui-Gon stopped to mourn his life's passing. I will never forget it."

Anakin nodded, though he did not understand. His greatest enemy so far in his life had been a slave trafficker named Krayn. When he had died, Anakin had not paused to mourn. Far from it. He had rejoiced in his death. It could only be good for the galaxy that such a terrible being had ceased to exist.

Something to meditate on in my next session, he thought. *I'll add it to the list.* The difference between Anakin's thoughts and Obi-Wan's lessons was sometimes more than he wanted to examine. It was a struggle to reconcile them.

"Why do you think the bounty hunter did that?" he asked.

"That is the crucial question," Obi-Wan said. "He preferred to end his life rather than meet his fate with Granta Omega. That should tell us something."

"It tells us that Omega is very powerful," Anakin said. "And very cruel."

"Yes, but there is more," Obi-Wan said, as though to himself.

Anakin wanted to stamp his foot in frustration. *What? What are you thinking?* But Obi-Wan did not add to his statement. He just looked wise and thoughtful, as usual.

"There must have been six bounty hunters, then," Anakin said. He counted them off on his fingers. "The bounty hunter with the Stokhli stick. Floria and Dane together. Mol Arcasite. Teleq. Hunti Pereg. And now this one. That makes six. Floria and Dane were wrong."

"Perhaps," Obi-Wan said in the same thoughtful tone.

Annoyed, Anakin spun on his heel and trudged off to find Floria and Dane. They had gone off the trail and had hiked up a small rise, where a space cruiser was nestled in a small hollow.

"We have a way to get off-planet," Floria said excitedly. "This must be his ship."

Anakin nodded. "Who was he? Do you know?"

Dane shook his head. "We were positive there were only four other bounty hunters. It was important for all of us to know exactly how many bounty hunters were involved. We all insisted on that. If Granta Omega had lied to us, we wouldn't have been happy. Even Omega wouldn't want beings like Hunti Pereg and Mol Arcasite as enemies."

Obi-Wan walked up. "It's time to leave Ragoon-6."

"The best words I ever heard," Floria said with a shiver. Night was falling. Blue shadows smudged the snow.

Anakin swung himself aboard the cruiser. He searched the cockpit, then motioned to Obi-Wan.

"Master, I found something strange. This cruiser belongs to —"

"Hunti Pereg," Obi-Wan finished.

"Yes," Anakin said. "But why is it up here, at the peak? Why isn't it the last bounty hunter's ship?"

"It is the last one's ship," Obi-Wan said. "That bounty hunter was Hunti Pereg. I am sure of it."

Anakin looked at him, puzzled. "Then who was the bounty hunter with the paralyzed legs?"

"It was not a bounty hunter. It was Granta Omega," Obi-Wan said softly.

Anakin was stunned. "How do you know?"

"Floria and Dane never met him, so they would not recognize him," Obi-Wan said. "Even so, he was in disguise. That synth-flesh I took for repair of an injury was designed to conceal his face. I realize that now. He does not want us to know what he looks like because he plans to meet us again."

"So he wasn't really paralyzed," Anakin said.

"No," Obi-Wan said. "That was also a ruse. He somehow knew that Floria and Dane had lied to him. He knew they were trying to trap him. So he came down to see for himself. He needed to be sure. When he saw us, he was."

"But how would he know? We were wearing laser cuffs."

"Young Padawan, if I can teach you one thing, it is this: Never underestimate an enemy. Or a friend. Now tell me. What did you think of the man you saw?"

Anakin thought back to the amiable bounty hunter with the paralyzed legs. "Not much," he said. "I mean, I didn't get much of a feeling from him one way or another. I got no sense of the dark side. Or the living Force, either, for that matter."

"Exactly," Obi-Wan said. "I have been thinking the same. There are beings that Jedi call voids. At first sight they seem to give off no real energy, rather like a hologram. But only beings with great power can project a simple blank to a Jedi. Sometimes a void can be much more dangerous than a being who pulses with the dark side of the Force. They are clever and focused enough to hide their dark side, and hide it so well they can even hide it from Jedi for a time."

"I didn't think Jedi could be tricked that way," Anakin said.

"Jedi can be tricked, my young Padawan," Obi-Wan said. "They can be wrong. They can make mistakes. Do not forget that. We try to minimize those things by following our feelings and connecting to the Force. Yet we are not infallible. Now, we must return to pick up Wren. Night is coming."

Obi-Wan beckoned to Floria and Dane, and the two started up the landing ramp. "Do you remember any details of Hunti Pereg?" Obi-Wan asked them. "What he looked like, or what he was wearing?"

"He was wearing white," Floria said. "I remember that. And he was tall."

"He wasn't very tall," Dane said. "But his face was very strange."

"Strange in what way?" Obi-Wan asked.

Dane frowned. "I can't remember."

"He had dark hair," Floria said.

"No, he had no hair at all," Dane said impatiently.

Brother and sister moved to sit down, still arguing. Anakin fired the engines, and the cruiser rose from the spot. He used the repulsorlift engines for planetary travel and cruised down the mountain.

He knew his Master was troubled. He could sense it. He was tired of comparing his Master–Padawan relationship with Obi-Wan and Qui-Gon's. He would always come up short. But was it fair for him to be angry at Obi-Wan because of that?

Ahead lay the snowy plain where they had first seen Granta Omega. No one was there.

"How could he have gone?" Dane asked, peering out the viewscreen. "The paralyzing dart couldn't have worn off so quickly."

Obi-Wan and Anakin did not answer. It was better that Dane and Floria still think that the man had been Hunti Pereg. Anakin slowed his speed and cruised over the plain. Within moments, he found what he was looking for. Below they could see evidence that a small cruiser had landed. Melted snow and scorch marks showed where the craft had taken off.

"Please land here for a moment, Padawan," Obi-Wan said. "I would like to examine the area."

Anakin set the craft down on the snow. He activated the landing ramp and Obi-Wan hurried down it.

Anakin stayed in the pilot's seat, watching Obi-Wan explore the landing site. Once again, he had been left behind.

CHAPTER SIXTEEN

Obi-Wan was disturbed. He felt queasy, almost dizzy. He searched through the snow, but he didn't know what he was looking for.

You don't know his power. It comes from the pyramid itself.

Obi-Wan had felt cold ever since hearing those words. The pyramid was a shape revered by the Sith.

The queasy feeling grew stronger. He remembered it well. He had felt it in the presence of the Sith Holocron. On that mission he had been disturbed by the Holocron's power. He had worried about Anakin's reaction to it. He did not want his Padawan to know what he suspected.

As if guided by his own unease, Obi-Wan reached down through the snow and put his hand on a small object. He pulled it out of the snow. It was a small black case.

He examined it, swallowing against the nausea that rose in his throat. There was no opening he could see, no seams. It simply appeared to be a cube.

He unsheathed his lightsaber and carefully cut a small seam in the cube. The case broke open. A small pyramid was nestled in black shimmersilk. It blazed to life, and he saw it was a holoprojector.

Unspeakable scenes flashed out at him, so quickly he could not absorb them. Murder. Suffering. Destruction.

Obi-Wan shut the case. He wiped the sweat on his brow. No, his Padawan must not see this.

"Master?"

Anakin had left the ship. He stood uncertainly a few meters away. "Did you find something?"

"It's nothing." Obi-Wan tucked the case inside his cloak. "We can take it back to the Temple for examination. Come, Padawan."

But Anakin did not move. "I need to know what you found. Don't you think I can feel it, too?"

He saw the sweat on Anakin's forehead, saw the slight tremor in his knees.

He could dismiss him. He could say, *You do not need to know.*

Would Qui-Gon have told him? Perhaps not. His Master revealed things in their own time.

Anakin met his gaze boldly. He would not back down. Obi-Wan saw that clearly. He would not allow the moment to pass. He would grab on to it, extend it, bend it to his will. He would do anything to obtain what he wanted.

He is so different from me, Obi-Wan thought again, bemused.

If he is so different from you, why do you treat him as though he is a younger version of you? Why do you act as you think Qui-Gon would have acted with you as his Padawan?

The question startled him. What was especially surprising was that he did not hear Qui-Gon's voice asking it. He heard his own.

Maybe it was time he stopped trying to be the Master Qui-Gon was. It was time to claim the role for himself.

"It is a Sith artifact," he told Anakin.

His Padawan swallowed. "I thought so."

"The bounty hunter mentioned a pyramid before he died. He said that Granta Omega drew his power from it. If the Sith are involved, or a Sith cult, that would explain much. The ruthlessness and cunning of the attack. The use of bounty hunters. The specific targeting of Jedi."

"Do you think Granta Omega is a Sith?"

"No," Obi-Wan said. "If he were, we would have known it. I think he is an ordinary being with a gift for concealment on a very deep level. He could have dealings with a Sith, or with a Sith cult. But he himself is not a Dark Lord. I think he wanted us to find this case. He wants us to know exactly how dangerous he is, and how far he is willing to go."

Obi-Wan gazed down the mountain and took in the lowering sky. Clouds rumbled, and snow suddenly began to fall, thick and fast.

"We have a new enemy, Padawan."

CHAPTER SEVENTEEN

Anakin put his hand on his lightsaber hilt. "I am ready, Master."

Obi-Wan raised an eyebrow at him. "Ready for what?"

"To go after Granta Omega." Anakin swallowed against the acid in his throat. The power of the Sith case was fading. He could face whatever Granta Omega would throw at them.

"We're not going after Omega," Obi-Wan said. "He's long gone. We'd never be able to track him through the galaxy."

"Never? One should not use absolute statements," Anakin said. One corner of his mouth twitched, a sure sign he was trying not to grin.

"It would be extremely difficult, then," Obi-Wan

amended with a small smile. "And we have a wounded Jedi to see to. Have you forgotten that, Padawan?"

"We could drop Wren at the Temple and retrace our steps," Anakin said. "We can't just let Omega go!"

"That's exactly what we can do," Obi-Wan said firmly. "Do not chase trouble, Padawan. There are not many guarantees in the galaxy, but I guarantee you this: Trouble will find you."

Anakin pressed his lips together. He did not agree with his Master's decision. They had stumbled on a powerful evil. Was it right to let it slip through their fingers? It wasn't like Obi-Wan to turn away from danger.

Unless he fears I cannot handle it.

Another doubt. They were crowding his mind on this planet. Was this the true purpose of the training exercise?

Obi-Wan knew how unnerved Anakin had been during their encounter with the Holocron. Perhaps he was afraid that Anakin would not be able to fulfill another mission dealing with the Sith or Sith followers so soon. He had almost not told Anakin what he had found. Anakin had seen that. Even though they had not encountered a Sith since the mission to Naboo, Anakin had been rocked by the dark evil of the Sith just being near the order's artifacts.

He is always trying to protect me. He does not trust me. What is the good of this exercise if Obi-Wan still doesn't have faith in me?

The thoughts crashed against his skull. Anakin tried to quiet them, to find the clarity of peace that Obi-Wan seemed to carry with him so easily, like a tool on his utility belt.

Obi-Wan slid the case into his cloak. "We will bring this back to the Temple and deposit it with the Sith Holocron. That will keep it safe. Now, let us return to Coruscant."

Wren was weakened but already beginning to re-cover when they returned to him. He was able to walk to the cruiser. They settled him inside, and Obi-Wan ad-ministered more bacta.

"We'll be in Coruscant by morning," he told him.

Wren gave him a wan smile. "I will be glad to see the Temple. This exercise did not go as I expected."

"Yes, you must be surprised," Anakin agreed with a straight face. "After all, I found you on the first day, just as I promised."

"I hardly think it counts," Wren said, drawing the blanket around his shoulders huffily.

"I don't see why not," Anakin said, flashing Obi-Wan a quick grin.

Obi-Wan grinned back. "I think we should let Wren rest. Maybe you should concentrate on piloting the ship."

They picked up the body of the Tursha and shot out of the sparkling green-blue atmosphere of Ragoon. The trip to Coruscant went quickly. Anakin admired the bounty hunter's sleek, fast ship.

"These sublight engines are tweaked," he said as he eased into a shipping lane on Coruscant at dawn. "Any chance we can confiscate this ship for the Temple?" He gave a quick glance at Obi-Wan. "Okay, okay. I know. We have to turn it in to the Senate."

"We have to turn in Floria and Dane, too," Obi-Wan said softly.

"*What?*" Floria had come up behind them. Her mouth was open, and her cheeks flushed pink.

"You broke any number of galactic laws," Obi-Wan said. "You tried to kidnap two Jedi. You sabotaged a cruiser. You —"

"But we helped you!" Floria protested.

"You didn't have much choice," Obi-Wan pointed out. "Don't worry, I'm sure the security authorities won't detain you for very long. They will try to place you with a family for rehabilitation."

Dane jackknifed to his feet. "Rehabilitation? Into what?"

"You will have a normal life," Obi-Wan said. "A roof over your head, schooling, a chance for a profession —"

"We are past wanting any of that," Dane said. "We have been on our own too long."

"What about your sister?" Obi-Wan asked. "Are you so sure it would not be better for her?"

Dane hesitated.

"Hey, I'm standing right here," Floria said. "And I want what Dane wants. He knows what's best. Not you."

"I'm afraid you have no choice in the matter," Obi-Wan said firmly.

They paused long enough to leave Wren at the Temple. They had called ahead so that a med team was waiting to remove him from the craft. Another Jedi came and carefully took the Sith case from Obi-Wan.

"Please inform Yoda that I will report to him shortly," Obi-Wan told him.

Obi-Wan directed Anakin to pilot the ship straight to security headquarters. There, they left Floria and Dane in the hands of a young security officer and left the body of the Tursha along with the scant information they had about him.

Floria leaned closer to the officer. "I'm glad to leave this life behind," she confided, her blue eyes very wide. "My brother and I regret the life we've led. We want to start over. Our dead parents would want it that way." Her eyes filled with tears.

Anakin rolled his eyes as the security officer led them off.

"This time, I can tell when Floria is lying," he said. "I think I've learned my lesson about pretty young girls with wounded eyes."

Obi-Wan smiled. "Floria and Dane will talk themselves out of detention, I am sure."

"So they will be on the loose again." Anakin shook his head. "They are too young for that life. Isn't there anything we can do?"

"No, Padawan. It is not our mission to save them. Beings take their own paths, and sadly there is little one can do to change that." Obi-Wan stood. "Come, let's leave the cruiser here for a moment. I want to see a friend nearby."

As they walked, Anakin marveled at Obi-Wan's detachment. He felt vaguely unsatisfied from the mission-that-wasn't-a-mission. They hadn't found the mastermind behind the attack on them. A Jedi was wounded and had almost been killed.

And as for the training exercise, in Anakin's mind it had been a complete failure. It had not strengthened the bonds of trust between them. It had done just the opposite. It had brought up questions Anakin did not want to ponder. It had made him question the bond it-self.

Obi-Wan indicated a café ahead. "This used to be Didi's Café."

"I remember Didi and Astri," Anakin said. "Did something happen to them?"

"Astri married a homesteader in the Outer Rim," Obi-Wan said. "She and Didi sold the café to Dexter Jettster and moved out there. I'll miss them. Didi introduced me to Dexter before he left. The first time I met him I didn't trust him, and now that I've met him a few more times I *still* don't trust him." Obi-Wan flashed a rare grin. "All I can say is that Dex is a character. Come and meet him."

Obi-Wan threaded through tables crowded with beings from all over the galaxy. He waved at Dexter, a large, four-armed and formidable presence behind the bar.

"Well, if it isn't Obi-Wan Kenobi. Glad to see you make an appearance," Dexter boomed. "I was hoping you'd still come around, even though Didi is gone. Naturally I will give you the same treatment." Dexter grinned hugely. "Except for the discount, of course!"

Obi-Wan laughed and pushed over a few credits. "This is my Padawan Learner, Anakin Skywalker. Some juma juice for the two of us. And some information."

Dexter deftly poured the bright yellow juice into two glasses. "Sure. If I have it."

"Have you heard of someone called Granta Omega?" Obi-Wan asked, pushing the juice toward Anakin.

Dexter frowned. "No. The name isn't familiar. I'll ask around, if you like."

"Thanks." Obi-Wan took a sip of juice as he turned to Anakin. "It was worth a shot. Dexter might have information for us one day. Then we will track Omega."

"And until then?" Anakin asked. He felt a little better. At least Obi-Wan was thinking of going after Omega at some point.

Obi-Wan pointed to Anakin's glass. "Until then, drink your juice." Obi-Wan waited until Anakin had taken a sip. "I owe you an apology, Padawan."

Anakin tore his gaze away from two odd species playing sabaac in a corner. "For what, Master?"

"You said I never share my thoughts. Instead of answering, I corrected you." Obi-Wan stared down into his juice. "It is not easy for me to share my thoughts, or my feelings. And sometimes it is necessary that I do not. When I was your age, I felt the same as you do. I thought Master and Padawan had to share everything."

"Don't they?"

"No," Obi-Wan said. "There are times when you do

not need to know what I am thinking. You must trust that I know best."

Anakin shook his head. "That's hard for me. I want to know everything."

"That is a quality I treasure in you," Obi-Wan said. "But it is also a quality you must learn to control." He gave Anakin a significant look. "There are things you keep from me, too."

"Not so!" Anakin protested.

"Midnight raids on junk heaps below the surface of Coruscant . . . a plan to build your own power converter . . ."

Anakin grinned. "Caught." He was starting to feel better.

He had worried that Obi-Wan did not have room for him in his heart. But Shmi's smile rose in Anakin's mind. *Hearts have infinite room, my son.*

It was one of her favorite sayings. Anakin sighed. He wished he could combine Obi-Wan's cool judgment with his mother's goodness. Someday. Maybe then his Master would trust him enough to let him tangle again with the Sith.

Perhaps he would never have a Master–Padawan relationship as deep and trusting as Obi-Wan had with Qui-Gon. Perhaps Obi-Wan kept him as a Padawan in order to fulfill a dying wish. But maybe it didn't matter how it happened.

He should not focus on what he didn't have. He had this. This was his. And that was something. He would work hard. He would be a great Padawan. And Obi-Wan would come to love him. He would make him do so.

"I think I know what you're thinking," Obi-Wan said, noting Anakin's sigh. "It was not the training mission I thought it would be, either. I thought I had things to teach you. Instead, you taught me."

"I taught you?" Anakin was surprised. "What?"

"That I am not Qui-Gon," Obi-Wan said. "And you are not me. Simple as that."

"Simple is sometimes best," Anakin said, repeating Obi-Wan's words.

"We are on a journey together, Padawan." Obi-Wan clicked his glass lightly against Anakin's. "We will forge our own path. Let us drink to that."

Across Dexter's café, someone watched the two Jedi. Someone with cool eyes behind dark-lensed goggles. Someone who had recently removed the synth-flesh that had knitted into his skin, leaving his skin raw. But no one looked twice at anyone else in Dexter's café. It was too dangerous and could provoke violence.

Go ahead, enjoy your drinks and your smiles, Jedi. You escaped for now. Yet I am not angry. I am only amused. It only gives me more time to play with you. You met me once, but you won't recognize me the next time. You'll look, but you won't see. You think I left the case behind by accident? I don't make mistakes. I just enjoy opportunities. And I make my own.

In other words, Jedi — we'll meet again soon.

ABOUT THE AUTHOR

JUDE WATSON is the *New York Times* best-selling author of the
Jedi Quest and Jedi Apprentice series, as well as the Star Wars
Journals *Darth Maul, Queen Amidala,* and *Princess Leia: Captive to
Evil.* She currently lives in the Pacific Northwest.

You know he became the most
feared bounty hunter in the galaxy

STAR WARS®

BOBA FETT

Find out how
he got that way.

STAR WARS®

ATTACK OF THE CLONES™

The Saga Continues . . .

Enter another galaxy with all-new *Star Wars* books from Random House!